A Fathers Wish

Howard L. Emmer

A Father's Wish

ISBN: 979-8-9910279-1-5 (Paperback)
ISBN: 979-8-9910279-2-2 (Hardcover)

Summary: A Father's Wish

Max wasn't listening to me, and I was at the end of my rope. This teenager was embarrassed by me, and I was devastated.

I didn't understand why I couldn't have the same relationship with my son that I had with my dad. My dad had been my best friend. We did everything together. Years later, when he passed, I experienced his last breath with him. We were mystically connected and I wanted desperately to connect with my son the same way.

I sat in my comfy chair like I had a million times before and meditated, as my dad taught me. I went fantasy traveling in my mind, hoping to find a pathway to my son - to reconnect more meaningfully.

"Help me, Dad," I pleaded.

Something miraculous happened—something so out of this world it was beyond explanation. Could this be what I was looking for? Would this be the miracle that would change my relationship with my son? God, I hoped so.

Read A *Father's Wish* to learn how never giving up on your child can create its own miracle.

A *Father's Wish* is the first book produced by Howard L. Emmer.

[1. Fiction 2. Fictional Fantasy 3. Teen & Young Adult 4. Boys & Men 5. Healing Story 6. Parenting & Relationships]

Copy Editor: Cindy Ziegelman Enterprises LLC

Formatting Editor: Cindy Ziegelman Enterprises LLC

Cover Design: Cindy Ziegelman Enterprises LLC

First Edition

CONTENTS

FOREWORD

By Max S. Emmer, Esq.

Fathers and sons have miraculously loving relationships – they are also complicated. This is the case for all parents and children. There is affection, adoration, love, and laughter, but there can also be sadness, stress, confusion, and criticism.

I was blessed with a one-in-a-million father—fortunately, I still am. Is he perfect? No, but who is? But is he my biggest advocate, admirer, champion, and supporter? Without a doubt.

My father taught me two things that few others can: (1) How the world really works and (2) How to connect with people. And for that, I can never repay him.

I often tell people that I am the 2.0 version of my father – more polished and refined, perhaps, but not better. Then, I wonder, maybe my son will be the 3.0 version. Thankfully, the Howard Emmer 1.0 version was and forever will be a glorious original. A one of a kind that deserves appreciation and celebration. A loving and adoring (if not sometimes annoying) father, a legendary salesman, a student of people and the human condition, and just an all-around good guy. We need more people like him in this world. Despite whatever I may say, think, or feel on any particular day, I will always be proud, privileged, and grateful to be my father's son.

Max and Howard at Niagara on the Lake

1

DISCONNECT

HOWARD

I am stubborn, just like my dad.

Unfortunately, after reflecting on my upbringing, I realized that my desire for control might stem from within. This led me to the current problem I found myself in — the relationship with my thirteen-year-old son, Max.

Before his teen years, we used to do everything together, from amusement parks to watching movies to sports to just chilling out together on the couch and talking. As he got older, I still wanted to be involved as he matured into adulthood, but I didn't know how. Even when I extended a helping hand, I was met with a "Yeah, sure," disregarding me altogether. How, then, did I learn the parenting skills necessary for engaging and mentoring my son without creating a more significant rift in our relationship?

It was a lovely night for a barbeque at the house. Just as spring ended, summer was creeping up on us, and the whole family was helping set the table. Max, my son, noticed the table was set for four and asked, "Who else is coming to dinner?"

"Uncle Dale is joining us tonight," I said, smiling. "It's just the four of us. Let's set the table, and we'll start the grill for burgers and dogs."

"How's practice been going?" I inquired, trying to get him to speak with me. I had tried numerous ways to approach him, but they were usually followed by, "It was fine, Dad." I'd heard another cold, defensive retort more times than I cared to listen. His barbs were rehearsed and designed to shut me up. My patience was running thin, but I persevered.

"How are classes wrapping up?" I tried again, delivering what I thought was an alternate path. *Here's to trying.*

"Good. Decent grades." There it is again—frigid. It's about to be summer, and he's living in the damn Arctic with these responses. Ilene, my wife, shrugged, indicating her annoyance with me.

"What the heck is going on between you two?" she whispered. I returned with a 'back me up here' glance. No dice. She wouldn't pull the pin on that grenade, and I don't blame her, but I could see her mulling over her response. This was my moment to run interference for her and redirect the conversation.

"Looks like your Uncle Dale is running a little late," I told Max. "While waiting, can you help me put the burgers and dogs on the grill?"

Max responded in his usual sarcastic, biting tone, "Dad, I am not eight years old anymore. We don't have to be attached at the hip. Why is everything a lesson with you?"

Ilene snapped, "Where is all this hostility coming from? Your dad wants to spend time with you." The proverbial grenade pin was pulled, and I instinctively stepped back from the counter.

Max sighed, gearing up for another round by avoiding eye contact like I wasn't there. His stare bore into her eyes, begging her to understand.

"I am thirteen. Do you see other fathers so obsessed with spending time with their children? I get it. He wants to teach me everything his father taught him, but I don't care. Plus, do you think Dad really needs my help making hot dogs and burgers? They're damn hot dogs and burgers! You don't have to be a Michelin chef to put cooked meat on the table!" His voice rose in cadence right up to his last jibe.

"I'm sick of this!" he screamed, stomping off to the other side of the kitchen.

There was the explosion I was waiting for, though it was more of a flashbang, stunning us into silence. We'd had tantrums before, but they were getting louder and more threatening every year.

Ilene and I sat speechless. You could hear crickets for a full minute before the doorbell sounded. Max jumped up as if he had been released from lockup and opened the door to see his Uncle Dale had finally arrived.

"Hey there, everyone! How's my favorite brother doing?" We had a bro-hug moment, and I bit my tongue as he moved to greet Ilene and Max. I still felt paralyzed by Max's toxic response, and Ilene bit her perfectly painted nails. Daggers were thrown via stares, and the tension was unbearable.

Dale shivered, "It sure feels chilly in here. Why aren't you speaking?" Dale filled the space with a chuckle, noticing the burgers and dogs still needed cooking. With only a nod and a smile to Max, the situation disappeared.

"Come, and I will show you how a master chef turns ordinary meat into magical meals."

Max was happy to join his uncle as quickly as he disrespected my attempts at bonding with him, and it hurt. The way he rushed outside to pal around with his uncle left a gaping hole in my heart. I didn't know if I would ever recover from it.

I finally shook myself from my stunned state and looked at Ilene with desperation and a sigh.

"Do you see how my relationship with Max is changing? He no longer needs or wants me around.

The way he pushes me away is so hurtful." I sat down at the kitchen table, exhausted from the exchange. "I wish I could turn back the clock to how things were."

Ilene nodded, endeavoring to recompose herself. "It's okay, Howard. He's a teenager. He wants to do things his way and not always your way." I knew she was right—she's always right.

I slumped back in my chair. I didn't know any other way to raise a son. I was never taught another way. The only way that I knew was the way that I was raised. What would I do if I couldn't connect with him how I wanted to? This was the moment that I committed to not giving up until I found a way to bridge the ever-growing gap between me and my son.

2

DISTANCE

MAX

It's never enough with him.

Spending time when it was socially acceptable was one thing, but having a parent hovering around or looking over my shoulder was frankly embarrassing. I wanted to have my own time. I wanted to learn who I was, not what he thought I should be. I also knew running away from my problems would only be a band-aid solution. Yet, I continued to run. When I heard the doorbell ring and saw Uncle Dale coming in, I knew that was my chance to hide behind someone who didn't chastise me.

"Come, and I will show you how a master chef turns ordinary meat into magical meals," he said. And, just like that, I found my way out of the middle of my parents' lambasting me. My way to survive was to remove myself from this smothering environment, even for a minute. I followed behind my uncle, relieved, and a smile crept up.

Uncle Dale looked back at me with a grin. I knew he would want to get the skinny on my life, and I was cool with that because he wouldn't interrogate me like my dad.

"Are sports going well?" I laughed as he juggled the platter full of meat and looked over his shoulder to get my attention.

"Yeah, I've been doing fairly good, though a few things are bugging me." I didn't want to get into the whole dad thing again. I'd gotten used to delivering small lies, half-truths, and hiding behind lies I told myself. Sadly, my situation had been bad for a while. And, unfortunately, it wasn't improving.

Uncle Dale snickered, "Ah, it'll be all good. You're a natural at sports!" He placed the dish next to the grill, bent down, opened the propane valve, and stood up. "Do you know the rest of what to do, or do you want me to show you?"

"I think I might need a refresher." I gave a slightly embarrassed chuckle. I had no idea how to turn this thing on the right way. That could be because Dad had been trying to teach me. In one ear and out the other. *Huh. Am I as stubborn as my father?*

Uncle Dale smiled and walked me through the process. He seemed happy being in his element. He pressed the built-in starter, and a burst of fire and heat erupted before settling into a flame perfect for grilling.

"Do you want me to put on the meat, or would you like the honors?" he offered. "Nah, I'll leave it to the Master chef. I'll help you move them around when they need flipping." I nodded to him, giving him the space to arrange the burgers and dogs as he wanted, inserting some flair as he managed the utensils, with a couple of tiny comedic fumbles mixed in. That master chef comment might not be all talk after watching him wield his flipper.

"I'm not like those characters you see on TV. I'm just an average barbeque-r with flair." A proud grin crossed his face, the exaggeration of skills seeming to bolster him. I chuckled at the joke and sat down on a folding camping chair. He sat down nearby and looked me straight in the face.

"So, what's going on between you and your dad?"

I sighed. There was no good way to answer that question. Instead, I delivered my rehearsed, put-together answer: "I can't have him always by my side, teaching and harping on 'how certain things must always be done in a certain way,' like his father taught all his children. I'm not his father's child but my own person." I sing-songed the speech like I'd said it a million times - and I had.

Uncle Dale nodded his understanding of what was happening—at least, I thought he did. He looked at the sky before responding.

"Max, your dad loves you and only wants the best for you. He's just...doing things how he knows how to do them. He is trying to get the same relationship with you that he had with his father. Most kids would kill for a father like him, someone who wanted to be close to them."

He paused, allowing me to process his words...and laughed.

"Speaking of someone close to you, now that you're thirteen years old, you got your eye on anyone?"

This man was clever, and I loved him for it. He'd always been a mentor and a best friend all at once. "Do you have any preferences? Girls your age? What about older ladies with FTBs?"

I laughed uproariously, "FTBs? What's that?" I asked, absolutely clueless about what he meant. I had some preferences in mind, but it seemed too embarrassing to say in front of him. He made a cupping motion at his chest like he was holding two big, ripe watermelons, "Full Titty Bras, kiddo. It's something your dad and I invented at your age."

"Pfft, Dad was part of making that? It doesn't sound like him." I grinned ear to ear. Finally, the tables had turned; I learned something about him, without him being the one to teach me.

"Oh yeah." Uncle Dale stood up and approached the grill to deal with the meat. "He was a bit *meshuggeneh* back in the day. He's mellowed out over the years, but I know he's still got that fun kid in there. One day, you'll appreciate his mannerisms and what he sacrifices to show you what a good father he is."

"Yeah, like that'll ever happen," I huffed, doubting his words. I stood up and went next to Uncle Dale, waiting for the meat to be ready. I assisted him while he took them off the grill, and he gave me a high five. I heaved a sigh outside, preparing myself to handle whatever crap Dad might throw at me. I only needed to take one step at a time to get through the next few days. *Summer camp, here I come!*

meshuggeneh—Crazy or wacky but used lovingly

3

A QUIET TALK

HOWARD

As long as Dale stayed at the table, dinner felt relatively normal, if a wall between one half of the table and the other was normal. Ilene and I were boxed out of the conversation— it felt lonely. The temperature cooled as Dale prepared to head out for the evening. I knew this chasm with Max needed to close sooner than later, but I doubted he would be open to discussing anything I had to say at any time. Dale was my only hope, and I didn't want him to leave until I got what I needed.

Dale gave Ilene and Max hugs and kisses as I watched, jealous of his ease and charm. He was effortless when conversing with Max, and the only difference was that I was his father, and he was his uncle. We both had the same dad, yet I was fighting to have a relationship with him.

When I heard "Goodbye," I caught Dale's elbow and whispered, "Hey, do you mind if I walk you out to your car?" Dale obliged willingly, waggling his eyebrow and smiling.

I patted him on the back. "Great," I said, following along. I looked back at Ilene for a second with a knowing nod before I pulled myself back into step behind Dale.

"So, what's on your mind, Howie?" he said, turning around and leaning back onto his car. That nickname had gotten old, but he still insisted on using it. From him, I didn't mind; anyone else had better not use it. I opened my mouth to speak, but he'd already continued with his observations. "I can see you and Max aren't getting along. Trouble in paradise? Isn't he enjoying your sage life lessons?" I blinked. *Huh. He hit the nail right on the head.* I guess it didn't take long for Dale to grasp the plot synopsis.

"Yeah...I want to spend time with him and give him the tools I was given to succeed." I sighed, and Dale chuckled.

He continued. "I get it, I get it. But there are a couple of things *you* might not get. For now, though, it's getting a bit late, and I have my things to do before tomorrow. I have a full morning. If you want to talk, I'll make time." Dale said, opening the car door. I reached out to him in a flash of desperation, and he stopped.

"I'm picking Max up early from school tomorrow for a doctor's appointment. I'll need to be finished by twelve-thirty. Can you make yourself available by eleven-thirty? I know I'm asking a lot, but I'm desperate to move our relationship to a better place." I'd need to move on to a professional if he had no solutions.

He sat down, buckled his seatbelt, shut the door, started his car, and rolled down the window. "Sure, works for me. Just...come with an open mind, okay, Bro?" He gave me a fist bump, giving me a reprieve from my thoughts.

"See you then."

"See you then." I grimaced before stepping back and letting Dale drive off for the night. This was a start. However, as he said, I needed to clear my head and have an open mind for our conversation to be helpful. I walked back inside, looked at the table, which had already been cleared, and shoved my hands in my pockets, resigned. Max quietly washed dishes by the sink as Ilene put the food away. When I walked in, Max quickened his cleaning and promptly headed upstairs, not wanting anything to do with me—not even a glare.

I've become a professional lamenter. After everything we've gone through, done, and seen, I still couldn't let it go. Ilene closed the cabinet, smacking it as it hit the frame and jolted me out of my stupor.

With a towel over her shoulder and a hand on her hip, Ilene inserted herself into my situation.

"So, how'd it go? Howard? Is there something you want to talk about?" Ilene said a note of irritation behind the words that told me all of this indirectly affected her—okay, directly.

I heard the stage calling, and this was the final scene of my Shakespearean tragedy: "Where did I go wrong? What did my father do that I haven't attempted?" I asked, sitting down with a thump. My hands clenched and unclenched as the stress got to me, but I realized that if I didn't breathe, this situation would kill me.

Ilene motioned for us to sit down at the counter island. "You've never mentioned much about your father to me and why what he said matters so much. Give me one of his sage lessons to hear how it might come across to Max." Ilene patted my hand and then placed her hands in mine. I pressed my lips together and considered her offer, then pulled my hands free, tapping my fingertips together.

What lesson should I discuss with my wife? Should I pick something I've been waiting to teach Max? *Probably. I'll call it a trial run.*

"My dad was a big sports lover. The most important lesson my father ingrained into me and my siblings was never to take on the weak. Dad knew the intricacies of sports psychology and made sure we found ways to apply those lessons to everything we did in life." I made a hand motion that I always remember my dad doing whenever he emphasized this lesson. Ilene chuckled.

I continued, "Now, that doesn't mean you can't respect the weak and play fair, but it does mean if you want to impact the field, you have to go after the biggest and strongest to show everyone who's the boss. The weak will be less of a problem after they know what you can do. We were taught to watch and learn from our opponents." Ilene's eyes widened, understanding the point.

Seeing the *oh* in her expression, I continued on an adjacent tangent. "I was always good at watching and dissecting every part of an opponent's strengths and weaknesses. If you go after someone's strengths and subvert them, all they're left with is their weaknesses. I would even play mind games with some of them, making them question whether their strengths were working." I was excited to share my pride in my father's wisdom and ability to process and apply it. It made me a fierce competitor in business and protected my family from being taken advantage of.

Ilene leaned in and kissed me passionately, something she hadn't done in a long time. "I'm so proud to be your wife, Howard. When you shared this story, I could see how it transformed you. Your eyes got big, and you smiled ear to ear. It reminded me of when we were young." Ilene pulled my hands into hers, threading our fingers just like when we were married.

"You know, if you share the full picture of why your lesson was important, I think he'd be more willing to listen," Ilene said, breathing deeply as she prepared to move on to the next part of the conversation.

"If he was willing to listen in the first place." My smile drooped as I felt the desperation creep back in again.

"We'll find a way to make him listen. Try and give him a reason to want to talk with you." She stood up, folded the towel on the counter, and turned off the light. This conversation was over, and I had a lot to think about.

My mind wouldn't shut off, and I replayed the whole evening, line by line. He won't listen to his old man. Maybe if I were the same age as him, he'd see me as a peer giving advice rather than an old goat. I shook my head at those words, not wanting to feel old but knowing that that was how the younger generation saw adults today. He'd rather have a friend give advice than his own father.

Ilene took my hand, and we headed upstairs. Being the sweetheart she was, she felt the need to console me one last time.

"Let's rest on it, ok?" she said, a feeling of fatigue spreading across her face.

"I think that's a good idea." I nodded. Maybe Dale would say something, anything, to work with.

4

ON THE FENCE

HOWARD

I t's morning.

I did not sleep well at all. Ilene could tell from the bags under my eyes it was a rough night. My reflection betrayed me as if there was more to me than a confused, tired, mildly desperate man. I had spent the whole night thinking about what to say, what to do, and if there was a correct way to do things. Unfortunately, all those introspective bouts fell short. All signs pointed to the number of mistakes I made while raising my son, and I couldn't help wallowing in my self-pity. I stared at the noticeable bags lining my eyes, an emerging gut, and a slightly bristled chin.

That wasn't the only thing I was thinking about. I was plotting on how I would reveal my situation to Dale. Which questions should I ask, and how should I ask them? More terrifying, what if his answers made me look like the bad guy? It was all so...uncomfortable. I felt the same way a kid would feel if they made a big mistake and had to tell their parents. My hands began to tremble, and I began to sweat, wondering if Dale would see me as a terrible father or, worse, not help me at all.

I needed to shake off my doom and gloom and get myself together. My son needed to be my focus, not whether I knew what the hell I was doing as a father. That was the past, and Max deserved my best, even if he wouldn't look at me. I didn't know if he felt bad, happy, content, or angry (probably angry, annoyed, and disappointed). I felt small having to ask someone to help me figure out what to do, but I obviously couldn't get a grip on this situation on my own. Hopefully, the conversation with Dale will lead to a meaningful discussion with Max and a solution that will salvage our relationship.

I skipped breakfast altogether and texted Dale that I was on my way. It wasn't a long drive to reach his home, but it gave me another twenty minutes to perseverate on what I would say to him; it didn't help he was standing on his driveway when I arrived. Ordinary people greeted each other when they got into someone's car. Not me and my brother, though. Our love language was minimal small talk with a certain passive aggressiveness that left us both feeling awkward. Today wasn't any different. The two of us had things on our minds, and I wasn't helping the situation because I was stalling.

I sighed, and Dale gave me one of his signature smug smiles.

"Need me to drive? You seem out of it?" he asked with a knowing look.

"It's alright. If I'm stubborn enough to keep my head on my shoulders for this long, I can make it to our destination." I gave him the same look back.

"Maybe that's part of the issue, Boychic." Dale pulled a "dad" on me and broke down my walls.

"You don't get to call me Boychic; that's Dad's word and, by proxy, my word." I retorted with a cheeky grin before I looked up and noticed the red light. I slammed the brakes, throwing us forward.

"Yeesh, I was joking about the driving, but now you're pushing it." He mumbled his concern, his eyes wild from the jostling.

I leered at him, "Tell you what, you can drive back."

"Deal."

I shouldn't have taken Dale to Max's school; it felt like spying. How else could I show him what Max experienced every day and that he didn't care that he wasn't the big kid on campus? It broke my heart that he wasn't picked first or picked to lead.

I found an empty spot near the chain link fences of the recess and sports fields to park at Max's school. Dale and I got out and walked over the hill surrounding the athletic area, just out of sight of any passers-by. Activities were starting, given the commotion I could see as I looked over the ridge. The chatter and laughter of the teens were a minor cacophony even from here.

"Where's Max? I know this is when he has lunch." I know he's my little Boychic, but when will I learn not to hover so much? I pulled myself up the hill in an army crawl, out of breath while I spoke.

"You've got Dad's face down to a T," Dale said, crawling beside me, his smug expression screaming I hate you for making me do this.

"What face?" I said incredulously.

"That face that said, 'That's my Boychic, my pride and joy.' And, given how much he worked, didn't have time to spy on us."

I blinked, remembering my dad's facial expressions, before giving a small laugh. "Regardless, I only have Max; that's enough, and that's why I have time."

"Having enough time to smother your kid isn't a good thing, Howard." Dale may have hit the nail on the head, and boy, did it hurt.

"If I had to go through this again with another child or more, I think I might break rather than bend," I chuckled, lying beside him on the slope. "I am worried for him, you know. He's small and thin and keeps getting picked last for games at recess. . ."

"I take it this isn't your first spy mission?" Dale interrupted. "Come on, man, Max has been putting in the effort. You just haven't been able to see it."

I had the decency to look busted. "I've seen a lot of it, and I just keep seeing him not getting his due." I felt like a balloon deflating into the hill, melding with the earth below me.

"Has it occurred to you that removing yourself from stupid crap like stalking him will help him feel better about himself? So, what if he's always picked last? He loves participating—end of story. The only one suffering is you. You need to trust him to figure out his stuff. He doesn't need his daddy following him around like a nut job. Give him time, Howard."

"You're right. I want him to have that special relationship with me that I had with our father. He's my little one, and he's the one who I want to be able to show what the world has to offer: everything big and small. He's my Boychic." I said, sinking even deeper into the ground. I could feel the deep layers of rock below me pressing against my spine, reminding me I should use mine. But then I noticed a devious smile crossing Dale's face out of the corner of my eye. He was up to something. I was sure of it.

"Yeah, I get it. I always saw how Dad adored you. He gave you all that he had so you could be successful. He gave me similar love, but you had more of it. Speaking of showing Max the world and all its mystical things, you never did get back to me about that skydiving excursion I brought up on your last birthday."

My face went pale. First of all, I had forgotten entirely. Secondly...

"My answer is still no way. You will never catch me jumping out of a tin can and plummeting to my death. The heights alone would give me a heart attack," I said exasperatedly. Dale looked over and began to howl with laughter, which was contagious enough to snap me out of my fear, and I laughed as well.

Dale smiled. "Glad to see I could get you out of your head, even for a moment." Dale nodded to me.

"I appreciate it. Now, how to go about talking to Max..." I said, my brain churning with questions.

"Take a night. Sleep on it. I'm hoping with time, you'll have a chance to ponder our conversation and find the answers you're looking for."

"Right. So, you're driving?"

"Yup."

"Fantastic."

5

FANTASY TRAVEL

HOWARD

Dinner was another struggle, but I did have a smile on my face, if nothing else. Things will work out. I needed to relax my brain as much as I could, hoping that today's conversation would bring realistic solutions. I had to believe they would. It'll all work out. *Hmm.* Max rifled through the pantry, looking for snacks and trying to find something to nosh on after another tedious conversation. *He was learning the fine art of stress-eating at an early age. Sorry, Boychic.*

I called over to Max before I mounted the stairs. "Hey Max, remember that fantasy travel thing I taught you? Have you used it recently? You know, the one for imagination?" I was grasping at straws, trying to rekindle a connection we had when he was young. After my earlier conversation with Dale, I felt confident and happy that this exercise would bring us closer. Max, however, didn't look enthused.

"Why would you bring that up now? Do you think I don't have an imagination?" Max's barbs split me in two as his defensiveness erected like a fortress. I sighed. I should have known it wouldn't be that easy.

"There's nothing wrong, and there's nothing to worry about. I was only asking if you would like to try it again."

Max shook his head, resigned. "Will it get you off my back?" He barked at me.

After hearing his loud accusations, Ilene poked her head in the room, giving Max an annoyed look, and walked upstairs to avoid further confrontation.

"Sure." I nodded.

Max moved like a sloth, head hanging low, and shoulders rounded on his way to the den, muttering as he went, "Better get that in writing. . ."

We had this great big chair where I got to relax and think. Reddish-brown leather, a seat big enough for my growing girth, and a kid that adored his father. It wasn't lost on me that my little Boychic was growing up, and that chair wasn't as roomy as it had been—another irony to ponder. I saw images of me holding a book in front of Max and reading to him or having our eyes closed and basking in the serenity of a quiet nap before Ilene called us for dinner. We'd playfully look at each other and snicker about the plane or car rides we were just on before we shuffled out of the den to eat.

If I could have a superpower, it would be to freeze my relationship with Max right before he hit puberty. The time when he appreciated my jokes and my stories and wasn't embarrassed about how much I loved him. Sadly, time was moving quicker than I could wrap my head around, and it scared me. The struggle to get the same imaginative, high-energy boy into the chair to take a chance on his dad's intuition wasn't changing. My doubts about improving our relationship were growing, but I wouldn't let that stop me. My den was a time capsule of memories, traditions, and promises. This had to be the place to make us whole again.

Max looked at the chair and stopped, contemplation on his face. It faded, and he whispered. "I don't know if both our tushes will fit there anymore."

"Yeah...we've kind of outgrown the double-seater setup." I laughed at my image of us trying to squish into the seat. "Take the helm, young sailor."

He shook his head, annoyance written all over his face, hidden by a knowing smile, and sat down. I circled the room to sit in a swivel chair, giving Max all the room he needed to move through the exercise without me breathing down his back and him not being able to see me watching him. Max closed his eyes and began to breathe deeply. In and out, going through each step to clear his mind, but something seemed off. He spent several minutes sitting there, his mouth twisting into a slight frown and teeth grinding. I didn't want to pry, but there was no time to do so, even if I wanted to. I jumped, confused, as the meditation ground to a screeching halt. His eyes opened, refocusing as if he had begun his mind journey, and pulled out quickly. *Did it scare him?*

"I'm done with this. You're always trying to control me. I'm not a kid anymore. This exercise is stupid, and I'm going to bed." Max stood up and bolted from the den toward the stairs.

"Wait..." I called out in futility. Another chance knocked to the side like paper in the wind. I felt as if Max was embracing this exercise again. Something I could latch on to. I left the den like Max entered it and slowly headed up the stairs for bed.

My head was reeling again, and it exhausted me. The fantasy travel exercise Dad taught me was an excellent tool I used growing up. When he added the breathing technique, it relaxed me even more, allowing me to work through my emotions. Max had to have experienced this, too, but he was so caught up in me asking him to do it that he got frustrated. I saw his smirk when he began. I saw that singular moment of connection I could latch on to, except now it felt like I was looking too hard in the wrong place.

There was more to this than I thought, so I set it aside for the night. I completed my nightly ritual and fell into a deep slumber.

6

EPIPHANY

HOWARD

"**E**ureka!" I shouted, shaking the house, no, the neighborhood.

The light that went out when I fell asleep figuratively lit again and shined brightly over my head. "That's how I'll do it!"

Ilene, who rested beside me, now stirred. My mishagas was taking its toll on her, giving her the same extreme bags under her eyes and worry marks on her forehead. "Howard, why are you shouting at this hour? Why are you even awake in the first place?"

"No time to talk. I need to call Dale." I grinned ear to ear like nothing in the world could stop me. My hand fumbled over my nightstand, locating my phone. I righted myself and walked to the bathroom, pounding his number on the keys. Ilene, in contrast, slowly sat up and padded over to listen to the conversation, even if she could only hear one side of it. The phone rang and rang and went to the answering machine. I immediately hung up the call and tried again. Ring...Ring...Ri–

"Howard! What the hell? Why are you calling this early in the morning?" Dale groggily sloshed out of his mouth.

"I figured it out." I pleaded. "I figured out what I need to do to connect with Max. It's obvious when I think about it." Ilene walked up behind me, confused as can be.

"Howard, what are you talking about?" She said with effort, still trying to get her bearings after being pulled from a deep sleep.

"Can't this wait till the morning? It's three o'clock..." Dale whined.

"Nope, it can't. I can't afford to forget the vivid dream I just had," I said, loud enough so that both Ilene and Dale could hear. The time didn't matter.

"What vivid dream?" was all I heard from both sides. I shook my head to screw it back on my shoulders.

I began explaining quietly, albeit with giddiness, "I was in bed resting, and suddenly, I heard a voice. I didn't know where it came from, but I knew who it was. It was Dad! I couldn't believe he was there. I got up and began looking around the house, trying to find the voice, yet it stayed in the shadows no matter where I looked. That was until I went into the den. In my chair, the chair where Max and I did our meditations, I found the voice. A mystical voice called out, telling me I could do something unbelievable, and my mouth spoke two words, 'I wish.' That's crazy, right?"

I looked over to Ilene, and silence filled the room. The feelings I had just experienced in my dream were heady and overwhelming.

With my phone in my hand, I approached Ilene.

"I've never spoken to anyone who had passed on. It isn't that I don't comprehend it could happen, only that it has never happened to me. I'd been so focused on trying to be like Dad that it didn't occur to me that the next best thing was to hear from him in a dream. Doesn't that make sense?" I was dumbfounded.

She replied, "I suppose it could be more than a coincidence, especially since you and your father synced up during that dream."

"Dad granted me a wish using his meditation technique, and I will use it." I continued my thought, and my excitement began to build.

Dale pushed through my revelation, saying, "You're out of your mind, Howard. A wish? That's insane to follow a 'hunch' like that, much less random dream messages that may or may not be fictional."

I wasn't taking no for an answer. "Maybe it could work? I always felt something magical happen when I practiced meditation. You won't know what I'm talking about if you haven't tried it."

I waited patiently for Dale to wrap his head around the situation. I didn't blame him; it was three in the morning.

"Hang on a minute, Dale," I whispered into the phone and turned to Ilene.

"Sweetheart, why don't you go back to sleep? I'll be back in bed shortly. We'll talk more later. Get some sleep." Ilene looked worried about my mental health. I didn't blame her. If any other person were saying this, she'd call a psychiatrist. She knew when I was serious about something, even if it was so far out there, you'd have to get a team of astronauts to go up into space to find it.

She sighed, "But, come back soon. You need your rest, and we must start planning what we're doing for your birthday in a couple of days." I nodded. If nothing else, I can do that for her.

I turned my attention back to Dale.

"Listen, I know it seems like I'm out of my mind but hear me out. If I make this wish, which fixes my relationship with Max, who cares what I look like? It's so crazy, it just might work."

Dale muttered a few parting words, and I hung up the phone and clapped my hands together like a madman. "It's time to make a wish."

It might be three in the morning, but the wish was calling, and I had work to do. I headed down the stairs as lightly as possible and went to the den. It didn't help that the floorboards creaked, and I had to turn on several lights so as not to kill myself, but I made it safely and began observing my surroundings.

Books, papers, and other bits and baubles were scattered about. It struck me how it resembled my mind these days—chaotic. Memories that had served me well covered every inch of those shelves. A baseball Dad and I caught at a major league game when I was eight, a picture of us walking through the Redwoods in Southern Cali, and my favorite, a hockey jersey my dad specifically bid on at a Temple fundraiser beating out David Green's dad. I hated that kid. Of course, a few bittersweet objects caught my attention, like the picture of us at a Chicago Bears game. Max was on his phone the whole time, and I took the worst selfie ever. I wish I could say that was a one-off, but it wasn't. I wandered over the hardwood to the chair next to the window. I reminisced about all the good times I had with Max, and my chest was filled with pride and joy. Every time we sat down to imagine together, we promised to make those dreams come true. I may have forgotten the power of imagination, but it was time to put it to the test.

I sat down in my comfy chair and nestled into the buttery leather. It was ironic how similar my chair was to my father's, although his was worn and needed refurbishing. Other things caught my attention like when I was here with Max yesterday: tax documents that needed putting away, little figurines on the shelves, pictures of the adventures I'd had with Ilene and Max, and the rest of the family. There were even some empty picture frames waiting patiently for future events. This was my holy place, and if I couldn't conjure up a miracle here, it wouldn't happen anywhere. I was blessed with *nachas* at each memory and also a little sorrow at my current disconnect with my son.

Breathe in, breathe out. Repeat. After several cleansing breaths, I intentionally breathed in an extra big breath, envisioning a blue sky above me in my mind filled with large white and fluffy clouds. Like hypnosis, I used visualization to use a big white balloon as a focal point for my breathing exercise. I would inhale deeply and exhale as hard as possible to push the balloon far away from my body. In and out, I made the balloon travel further and further away. A peacefulness fell upon me: rhythmic, stabilizing, centering. I gathered my thoughts and fine-tuned their intent. Every word and feeling brought my body calm and light until my body spoke to my mind, freeing it from this plane. Suddenly, I was sitting in a white room across from my dad. He didn't say anything, only gave me a soft smile.

He looked like he was just before he passed: wizened, mindful, and always with softened sternness.

"Dad. . ." drifted from my mouth, my breath was stolen for a moment. I tried to stand up from the chair to go to him, speak to him, share everything left unsaid, and how I missed him. I reached out, but instantly, he was gone. I didn't know whether to laugh or cry at this phantom figure. It was so real and made all those feelings of loss pierce my carefully erected emotional walls.

I blinked. Did...did that happen? Oh my god, that just happened. Ok, no time to get giddy. *Well, maybe a little.* I did it. I DID IT! I did a happy dance in the chair, quietly cheering for myself before restarting the meditation process once more. Thankfully, I was able to do it again. I could see him. I could make my wish!

A minute of meditation passed before I returned to the white space. Once again, my dad was across from me. Silent, with understanding eyes and a self-satisfied look that I hoped meant he was happy to see me. This was a dream come true!

I gathered my courage and spoke slowly, "I don't want to assume anything, so is it true? Can I make a wish, and you'll grant it?" He was quiet, but a slight nod of approval gave me the assurance I needed to move forward.

"Okay, let's do this," I said nervously. I had heard nightmares about people not being precise about their wishes and receiving something wildly different.

I closed my eyes, pin-pointing every word precisely to get my wish delivered accurately.

This was it. There was no going back, and I highly doubted the universe would offer another opportunity.

"I want to connect to Max better, but I don't know how. I don't know how to be his friend, confidant, or mentor in the way I want to be. I want the same kind of relationship I had with you, Dad. But he doesn't want a father like you. Honestly, he doesn't even want me most of the time. What if I connected with him more like a peer than a parent? Yes! That's what I wish for. I'd be able to spend time with him so he can get to know the real me...and hopefully, our relationship will improve.

I took one more big breath and proclaimed my wish to my dad. "I want to be Max's age for thirty days alongside him at summer camp. That way, I can be his peer, and be a friend, and help him if anything goes wrong." I nodded and then opened my eyes. When I did, my dad was nowhere to be seen, leaving me alone in a void of white. I blinked again and found myself in the den, sitting in my incredible chair. I shook my head. Was that a hallucination? Was Ilene right? This was more than a coincidence.

I didn't feel any different, and after checking on Max, nothing had outwardly changed. Before Max went to camp in a few days, I had to know if my wish worked. Nervousness ate away at my confidence, and

I hoped this didn't turn into a Genie in The Bottle situation, me being stuck with the consequences of my hare-brained idea. I headed quietly upstairs to sleep and prayed something good would come from this wish. The idea that my relationship with Max could get any worse terrified me.

   *mishegas—craziness; senseless behavior or activity
   *nachas—pleasurable   pride   in   another's achievements

7

A FATHER'S MIRACLE

HOWARD

Two nights later, anxiety crept in, and my hopes for this fantasy dwindled every minute. I don't know when, and I don't know how, but I could feel the vibrations in the air changing. Too bad I had to wait to contemplate it until later—today was my birthday!

I always enjoyed planning parties. Choosing the food was easy. I loved to eat. The guest list, however, could get dicey, especially if I mixed up my friend groups. Family was family, and they had to be invited, although if a few begged off, I wouldn't have my nose out of joint. I won a thirty-dollar bet with Ilene that my sister, Karen would cancel at the last minute. Her excuses ranged from "Oh, I forgot", to "I have pneumonia." It's the easiest thirty bucks of my life. Either way, she always sent a great gift.

Max stayed hidden, even though I would have loved his help setting up. Ilene pulled dinner out of the oven, and the smell of potatoes and brisket permeated the house with a wonderful scent, keeping me focused on my party. The doorbell rang, and our first guest arrived—early. There was always one person who couldn't wait to get things started.

Max shouted, "I'll get it!"

A minute or so passed, and Max came over, dropping a package on the counter in front of me. "Dad! An older man came with a package for you. He just handed it to me and left."

Strange men dropping boxes off at my door should have been a red flag. My son answered the door to strangers; strangers had definitely been there as well. I pushed down the urge to chastise him about it but given the wild things that had happened over the past forty-eight hours, I let it go. I then redirected my interest to what was in the box.

"Thanks, Max. I'll check it out in a while. In the meantime, please put the glasses on the table." I tried keeping my tone easy-breezy, but again, Max replied with a cool gust.

"Fine, I guess so."

I smiled. "Thank you, son."

With those three words, I casually headed back to the door and whipped it open, wondering if I could see the man who dropped my package—no such luck. I returned to the kitchen, hefted the box on my hip, and entered my den. The box was sizable, wrapped in blue gift wrap dotted with stars across the wrapping. Underneath the bow was an envelope with my name on it. Whoever dropped this off may be a stranger, but they knew enough to put my name on the card. I gently pulled the white envelope off and turned it over a few times, wondering again if it was safe. The oddest thing was that I recognized the handwriting—it was my dad's!

Was this it? Was this the thing I'd been waiting for? I frantically open the envelope, recoiling when I lanced myself with a paper cut before diving back in and pulling out the card. On the front of the fold was a party hat with the words, "It's your birthday! Make the most of it!" emblazoned in a curly font. A card from beyond the grave for my birthday meant much more, considering what might be inside it.

I opened the card first to see the printed words typed by whatever quippy wit a writer thought up that day. "Enjoy another year being the best you!" I grunted. The best me at the moment meant *bupkis* if Max and I couldn't get it together. I flipped the card over and found a note in my father's handwriting, tripping me out again.

Howard, my Boychic,

I see you are struggling with your son and have called on your old man for help. You want that similar connection you had with me, and that warms my heart. I know you're not always one for shortcuts, so this wish comes with an option. The next time you open this card, you will become thirteen again for thirty days, enough time to enjoy camp alongside your son as his peer and not his father. The last and final time you open this card, you'll return to being your adult self.

As I mentioned, this opportunity could lead to the student becoming the teacher, so beware. You might be the one getting the lesson, not Max.

There is a small caveat. You should remember that wherever you are, at the end of thirty days, you will change back to being an adult. This is a miracle for you and also a shortcut. It's up to you if this decision is right for your relationship. I know you'll make the right choice for yourself, and I'm proud of you either way. I'm not made of miracles, so don't rush into this decision. If you decide to open the card again, have fun at camp. Sorry, I never sent you when you were a kid.

All the love in the world, Dad

Tears welled in my eyes as I read the words on the card. They weren't tears of sorrow, well, not most of them. They were tears of hope. He was right. I am taking shortcuts. Perhaps I should consider a different path. However, I am me. Once I set my intention in stone, that becomes my path. As I mentioned before, I am stubborn, just like my dad. I wiped my tears, grabbed the package, and spirited the box away into a place where Max wouldn't look for it. Before I returned to the dining room, the first actual doorbell of the party rang throughout the house.

The day after my birthday, I contacted Camp Windy City to apologize for the late camper application. I would now be known as Larry Pit, a name that had many meanings. Lawrence, a.k.a Larry, was my middle name, and Pit came from a nickname I earned during pee wee football. Hence the name Pitbull. I was muscular and stocky, with no neck, all shoulders, and my bite could match any bark the other players could give. After my call, I secreted off to open the package my dad sent. As I suspected, he had provided all the necessities a thirteen-year-old would need for camp life. Thank goodness I saved a cool T-shirt from when I was young. It was red, with the nickname spelled out in big white block letters across the chest. This was my go-to shirt whenever I needed to feel like a warrior.

I covered up my secret life by talking to Ilene here and there about her legal case at work. She'd been stressing about it for a few weeks, and soon, it would go to court.

"I wasn't lying about this deadline, Howard." Her exasperated tone implied I hadn't been paying attention to her enough. *She was right.*

Ilene was a family law attorney who took her cases to heart. I respected her for her work as an attorney and hoped this case went well. I knew she had a lot on her plate leading up to Max going to camp, and adding another burden, me, might put her over the edge. Ilene and I loaded our car with Max's duffle bags and met the bus at his school.

Today was the day my life would change. School was over, and Max was packed. He was chomping at the bit to go to camp, and so was I. In the past, he would let me walk him through a camp checklist, ensuring he didn't forget anything. Not this time. He pushed me out of his room, telling me he wasn't a child anymore and he wouldn't die if he forgot something. I didn't think he would die, but let's face it, a month without shoes would be a big problem. Instead, I was making a checklist in my head of what not to forget to pack. Max might not die, but I was an adult in kid's clothing and didn't want to be uncomfortable all month.

We arrived at the school, and Max sprung out of the car and into his mother's arms, confirming my intuition—he was running away from me. He barely patted me on the shoulder before turning and throwing his duffle bag onto the growing pile by the bus. I reached out instinctively, hoping that he would look back, but he gave no fanfare, hugs, or good wishes; he only hopped on the bus and left. *Just wait, Max. Things are going to change for us.*

It was a sad, lonely ride back to our house. Neither Ilene nor I could find the words to describe how cruel Max had been by not even speaking to me when he left. We entered the house, and Ilene put the kettle on for tea. I sat at the kitchen table quietly, wondering about our predicament.

"Did he say anything to you?" I worked up the courage to ask Ilene. Her response was less than stellar.

"Where did we go wrong? How horrible is his life that he couldn't even look you in the eye and tell you he loves you?"

"At least he hugged you and said he'll see you soon. I got nothing." I sounded like a whiney brat, but I was sick of getting the raw end of my son's attitude.

Ilene placed her hand on my cheek in consolation.

"I think this time apart will be good for both of you. Take heart, Howard. Max's puberty will end one day, and he'll grow out of all these attacks."

"I hope so," I said dejectedly.

I wanted to stay and hold my wife in her comforting arms, but I had my own Mission Impossible movie to create. Now was the time to break the news to Ilene that I was leaving for a month. Every word mattered in this deception, and I hoped my delivery was convincing.

"Honey, I hate to bring this up, especially since Max just left for the month, but I figured since you were up to your eyeballs in this case and would be for weeks, I planned an extended golf excursion. And, since I'd already be traveling, I'd call on some potential business on the East Coast. I'll check in, but I don't want you to worry about me. Take all the time you need to knock this case out of the water, and then spend a few days at a spa to rejuvenate. I'll be home before you know it."

I was out of breath but pleased with my monologue. I hoped she went for it and my lack of attention to her this next month wouldn't be construed as neglect.

She gave me a sideways glance, her hand motions shooing me away. "Don't worry about me. I suppose all of us being alone for a month is healthy, if not lonely. Make sure you bring your meds and the small first-aid kit in the back of the linen closet. I don't want you to hurt yourself without a band-aid."

I stood up and kissed her forehead. "Thank you, sweetheart. I appreciate your support. I'm sure this trip will clear my head of all our recent troubles. Why don't we go out for dinner tonight? Maybe catch a movie?" She stood up and kissed me, alleviating me of my guilt.

"I'd love to go on a date, Howard. It's been far too long." She gave me a wink and walked towards her office.

I may have decided to proceed with my transformation, but I knew Ilene wouldn't be on board. I'd been ruminating on how I could best deceive her without being cruel. In our twenty-two years of marriage, we had only been apart for a week at a time. Thirty days was a lifetime when it came to a marriage, and I didn't want her to think I was leaving her.

I spent the rest of the afternoon making voice messages my brother Dale would send from my phone while I was gone. For a second, I considered sending them myself, but hell, I had barely hit puberty at Max's age. What if my voice cracked? Or worse, I sounded like a little girl! Ilene was forgiving, not stupid. This whole charade would be blown wide open.

This adventure needed careful planning. I had resolved to make this charade work, but I wasn't so selfish that I didn't need anyone's help.

Messages were completed, and I switched to spy mode. *Bum, bum, bum, bum, ba-ba, bum, bum, bum* played in surround sound in my head. The theme song from "Mission Impossible" had me leaping around the room, grabbing miscellaneous things I thought would increase my creature comforts while away. I even grabbed my Bears' baseball cap, remembering all the great memories I had as a kid watching football with my dad. I shoved a couple extra sweaters in my bag, and, bam, I was done!

The trip across Illinois to Camp Windy City would be filled with anticipation and, if I'm honest, some trepidation. What if Max still hated me? What if I got caught up in my web and couldn't escape being a teenager?! None of that mattered. I was so pumped up that I was out of breath running down the stairs and ditching my suitcase in the garage before Ilene suggested Italian for dinner. *What a way to go!*

Today was the day that would change my son's and my life forever, and nothing would stop me. I used the excuse of taking out the trash to throw my luggage and golf clubs on the driveway, hoping to keep Ilene from seeing a duffle bag alongside my suitcase. Conveniently, Dale had pulled in, and I motioned him to grab my stuff and throw it in his truck in case she wanted to walk me out.

I planted my hands on my hips, expelled a big gust of air, and stepped in closer to Ilene sitting on a barstool. "That's it, Ilene. I'm ready to go."

I spun her around, gave her a big reassuring smile and a tight hug, and turned towards Dale, standing on the other side of the counter, looking smug and excited.

"Have a good month!" I whispered into her ear as I squeezed her tightly. "I'll be back before you know it!" followed by several kisses.

She smiled at me, looked out at Dale, and said, "Keep him in line. Got that?" she teased.

We started my adventure like two kids with their parents' credit cards.

"Believe me, he will keep me out of trouble!" Dale shouted. Thank goodness Dale was on board with my crazy plan. He was a significantly better liar than me. I hopped in the passenger seat, knowing nothing would ever be the same from this moment forward.

bupkis – little or nothing. A worthless amount.

8

PEER

HOWARD

"You believe that this birthday card thing will work? You can say you had a spiritual realization and come back from the golf trip early." Dale queried, eyes trained forward, focusing on the highway.

I nodded. "Dad is granting me a wish. He'll come through."

As I looked out the side window, the expansive blue sky above was a perfect replica of my meditation sky, and a feeling of warmth and calm trickled through my body. Max had been gone just over twenty-four hours, and by the end of today, I could follow him around and know exactly who he was.

Dale gave me one of his sarcastic side-eye glances, "Why were you dad's favorite? I was the oldest."

"Dad told me he tried to teach you what he had taught me," I said, a little bewildered.

Dale scoffed, "What meditation?"

"You know, the one for fantasy travel." My attempts to trigger his memory fell flat.

"I was eight years old, and kids don't find it fascinating to meditate with their father. Where was my fantasy travel? Oh, wait, my fantasy travel was Dad yelling at me to get off the couch and turn the channel on the television. I was his personal remote control. So much fun." He said sarcastically, gesturing abruptly with his hand jutting towards the windshield. "In addition, on the most "special" so-called fantasy travels, he demanded I stop in the kitchen to get him a cold drink. I suppose his idea of fantasy travel through the Mojave Desert to find a cold drink began with me being his valet and him keeping his ass parked on the couch." He sighed.

When I was young, my experience with fantasy travel was described in one way. Still, as I grew older, the explanation expanded into greater detail about how meditation and deep breathing could relieve stress, bring immediate peace, and improve overall health. Before my father's passing, his final direction, if I ever needed it, was that I could reach out to him through mediation to feel his spirit, thoughts, and guidance.

When I was born and took my first breath, Dad told me I became a piece of his heart, and no matter whether he was alive or dead, that would never change. I knew I was loved deeply by my parents, but there was something deeper that my father and I shared that continued to be beat inside me. I could literally feel him in my heart and my head when I had big decisions to make. I took comfort in knowing he wasn't far away, though the physicality of his hugs was desperately missed.

Dale would never have the same relationship with our father as I did. We were two different people, but I wanted to share what I was going through.

"I know it's hard to comprehend, but I have been practicing his meditation plan since I was young. When I sit in my chair and go through all the steps, I can feel the hair on the back of my neck and notice a chill throughout the room. I can sense him and feel his love." I reflected, decompressing from the emotions this conversation brought up. Dale rubbed his forehead, listening carefully.

"You really are his Boychic." He looked at the GPS: "We're about forty-five minutes from the camp. Several gas stations are ahead, so pick your poison and begin your miraculous transformation."

I chuckled. "Mock me if you must, but I'm positive this fantasy will work. Don't you think that this body, shrinking to that of a thirteen-year-old, will take a little getting used to? I'm excited and freaking out as well, so you better be supportive when it happens." I chastised.

"Fair enough." Dale had the good sense to look remorseful. Several signs appeared on the highway, giving us directions to a multitude of gas stations and eateries. My wish was becoming all too real. Was I ready? What if this was a terrible mistake?

Dale barked, "Ten minutes, Howard." All thoughts of backing out went out the window. "We need to be at camp on time for your first full day, so you better tell Dad to move it along." He chuckled. "Why am I the one keeping you on task when it's your plan?" He mumbled.

I laughed, "Because you have your head on your shoulders more than I do. Give me a break. I'm under a lot of pressure here."

"That I can agree with. Now get yourself inside and do your magic."

I walked inside the gas station and looked around, those tingling feelings becoming more intense. It was a typical roadside place with a small restaurant attached to it. If we had more time, I'd sit down to a nice meal, enjoying what was coming. Instead, I fingered my magical birthday card, found the bathroom on the other side of the mart, and locked the door. I took one last look in the mirror and prayed I was making the right decision. I had to remember I could take any ridicule, just so long as my son was accepted by his peers. Carefully, I opened the card and immediately felt my body morphing. Every breath I took sent me into the same mind space as if astral projecting into a form from long ago. In and out, I breathed, pushing that figurative balloon further and further away until—my eyes opened.

"Ah—ah—" I tried to speak but recoiled as my voice cracked and gurgled. I completely forgot the sounds a pre-pubescent boy made as his voice dropped. "Oy!" I groaned. "This will take more than a minute to get used to."

I was the Incredible Shrinking Man from a 1957 Sci-fi movie. Each time I looked in the mirror and down at my body, my brain sizzled, and my body spasmed. It worked. It worked! Wahoo! Yes!

My whole reduction lasted less than three minutes, and the moment my brain calmed and my body settled, I realized my next problem.

"Oh, crap!" I hissed.

Giant-sized clothes hung off me, and my pants hit the floor with a clang sounding from my belt buckle. It was good that my dad had the forethought to send a month's worth of clothes, though I couldn't understand how he knew my size once I shrunk down. I could feel him as he smacked his thigh while laughing hysterically at how funny I looked donned in my man clothes. "Thanks, Pops. Don't have too much fun with this transformation."

I opened the bag I had brought and changed into the appropriate camper clothes and a thoughtfully scuffed-up pair of tennis shoes. I stuffed my old clothes into the bag, looked at myself one last time, and gave myself a pep talk.

"Let's go! Let's do this!" I fist-pumped the air and ran back to Dale's truck.

He was deeply engrossed in his phone when I jumped into the passenger seat. With a loud burst of energy, I screamed, "Hey, bro!" He startled for a moment, blinked, and pinched himself.

"Uh.... oh my God, it worked. Geez, Howard. How are you feeling? What did it feel like? Where is the card? Don't lose that, idiot."

After his onslaught of questions, he gave me a small 'ha!' and threw his truck in gear. We only had five minutes to go, and I needed every minute to "fit" into my new body.

"Hey bro, why don't you ask Dad about the lotto numbers? We could make millions with this kind of power." Dale's look of excitement didn't deter me from my quest.

"Nah, nah, nah. This is Dad we're talking about. He'd never let us shortcut life that way."

"You say that, but look at you! I mean, come on. You've got to at least let me get a picture of this."

"Not a chance."

"Please!" He lifted both hands from the wheel, pressing them together in prayer.

"No way! Not like this."

Like a peasant to his king, "C'mon, man, just one, I beg of you, oh great and mighty wielder of miracles!"

There was a little twinge of pride at his remark—*great and mighty wielder of miracles*. I'd better keep my feet on the ground and not let comments like that go to my head. But because I felt like a thirteen-year-old stinker, I indulged him.

"Fine, fine. One time. But you can't send it to people who would send it to Ilene or Max, and once you send it out to whoever you want, throw it away. I don't need you having that kind of power over me." I made a finger gun and jerked it twice for effect.

"All right, all right." When we stopped at the sign outside of camp, he aimed his phone at me and took a picture, "Are you really you, but thirteen?"

"Yeah! Crazy, right?"

"Insane. Are you afraid that the government will take you for testing or something if you get found out?"

"Change of plans. You can't send that picture to anyone connected to government workers."

We both laughed. "Agreed. Now, let's get baby brother to camp." He chortled, pulling through the camp gates. "You are one crazy bastard."

9

LARRY PIT

MAX

The trip to camp was long and boring. I remembered a few kids from last year but didn't start making conversation immediately. I was still miffed at my dad for being so controlling over everything that I did or didn't do. I felt relieved to be myself for the next month and hoped I would learn new tricks to get him off my case.

Once I got out of my head, I sat back and closed my eyes, listening to everyone's conversations, wondering what drama I had to look forward to. I heard gossiping about the past school year riddled with annoying sports stories about the jocks, the high drama with the "in" girls, and which teachers to avoid next year.

The bus stopped, and we all herded off one by one. As we made our way to the side of the bus, I slid through gravel to retrieve my duffle bag. Before I knew what was happening, a stampede of kids rushed from behind me, knocked my backpack from one shoulder to across my back, and then plowed me into the ground in their rush to the mess hall. I got that they were hungry, but did they have to knock me over to get there? *This better not be a premonition of things to come.*

I knew the hazards of being a small kid. I made it a point not to be around anyone more than three inches taller than me—with a few chosen exceptions. Unfortunately, those hulking gorillas would be a part of my summer, and I needed a plan to steer clear of those self-centered apes.

I got up from the ground, swatting away dirt and leaves, and noticed my knees were scrapped. *Great!* I'm not here five minutes, and already I'd managed to hurt myself. If it weren't for the few friends from the past years slated to be in my cabin, I would have trekked off to the infirmary. I made it a point to focus on meeting up with my camp friends and the few school friends at my camp session inside the mess hall.

The first day was always the same: meet your cabinmates and your counselor who drilled all the rules into you—again, then Flagpole, to learn a couple of camp songs, finishing with boundaries. Now that we were thirteen this year, we could stay up later and hang out with the girls longer. I wasn't sure I was ready to experiment with a girl yet. But maybe a tiny kiss?

I barely had time with my friends before lights out. However, our counselor put together a game that he thought was cool.

"Okay, kiddos. Here's the boogie from your bunk; you'll have to pick a shape, a circle, or a square, and then be given a question. If you picked a circle, you could spin your answer off the person before you. If you picked square, you'd start a new thread of answers. Capice?"

We all mumbled, "Capice."

Two kids went before me, and I liked how their answers sounded, so I picked a circle.

"Max, here is your question: Who in the world would you least be interested in their opinion?" My counselor, Dave, sat back calmly in his chair, leaving his note cards precariously on his thigh.

I struggled to remember the previous responses and then had to think of my answer, but it dawned on me, and I sat up straighter.

"I'd ride my elephant, which I stole from the zoo," Evan answered when asked what animal he would steal from a zoo.

"And strap him into a Ferris wheel," answered Jacob about his favorite carnival ride.

Then it was me. "And never ask my dad for permission to go to the carnival in the first place." *Wow! That was telling.* Now, everyone knew I hated my dad's opinions. *Did I hate them? Or was it because I hated that they came from him?*

It didn't matter; everyone laughed and agreed their dads had been riding them, too. *Hmm.*

Morning came quickly, and my cabin huddled together in the cool breeze. Before I entered the hall, I noticed the camp director speaking off to the side with a kid I didn't recognize. He was probably a newbie trying to find his groove at what presumably was a new camp for him. He looked around my age, except he looked like a miniature pro football player. Hopefully, he wouldn't be another jerk like those jocks I had to deal with last year. With those sobering doubts, I turned and walked in to meet my friends.

Silverware clattered against plates, and footsteps clumped throughout the hall. Not that I had any experience myself, but between the gossip of the girls' tables, the raucous noise of the boys all laughing and shouting about their recent school exploits, and the distant sounds of the kitchen firing on all cylinders, this could have been a prison, not a gaggle of teenagers. Not that I know anything about that. I loved this sound! I looked forward to it, knowing I could blend in and listen to all the good and bad stuff going on with everyone. I wasn't always like this. Honestly, I'd been highly overwhelmed during my first year. A fact I noticed even more acutely was the stunned silence of the kid I saw earlier talking to

Sid, the camp director. Now that I got a good look at him, this kid held himself with a little more confidence than I gave him credit for. It didn't matter how much confidence or his size; he would be a prime target for the jocks.

Like I summoned the wolf myself, the head jock of the camp, Greg, came over to the new sheep luring him into his den of corrupt assholes. I don't blame Greg. This kid looked the part with his muscular upper body and athletic build. He was probably a star athlete that would be a perfect addition to the jocks' ranks.

Wait! What's this kid doing? I openly gawked at this kid's subtle defiance by shaking his head and turning his back on Greg. I ignored my food and positioned myself closer. He was insane—delusional. You don't just say no to a guy like Greg. Even his buddies sat motionless, watching this conversation. Didn't this newbie know you'd get eaten alive confronting guys like Greg? I almost choked on my saliva as he casually strode away from him and towards my table, leaving Greg in stunned silence.

"Holy shi-..." I cut myself off mid-thought as he arrived. Flabbergasted and impressed at this kid's presence, I took a chance to speak first.

"Who are you?"

"Hey! Nice to meet you, I'm Larry Pit," he smiled wide. There was something familiar about that smile, but I couldn't put my finger on it. The confusion and shock of the whole situation made my mind reel.

"You talkin' to me?" I said, bringing the entire New York accent of Robert DeNiro in line. Of everything my dad taught me, using movie quotes to break the ice was the best education he gave me. This was one of those situations, and I wouldn't let it go to waste.

"Yeah, I'm talkin' to you." *Awesome!* You have to love a guy who communicates through movie one-liners.

"My name's Max. It's nice to meetcha," I said, settling myself so as not to act like an idiot. God, this must be how Dad felt after our arguments. He had that shocked expression, too, so now I was taking a play from his playbook again.

"Nice to meet you, Max. Hey, I was told by the camp director that I was going to eat with this cabin. He asked one of you to show me around the camp. Do you think you or one of your buddies here can help me out? As you can tell, I'm new, but I don't want to get in the way of you catching up with your friends." He looked a little embarrassed. I looked back to my friends, who had been talking between themselves, while I focused on the display near the door. They shrugged, and I returned my attention to Larry.

"Fine, I guess I can help out. Let's get going."

With my friends, we grabbed our stuff and dumped all our bags in our designated cabin.

"Hey, guys. I'm going to show the new kid around camp. I'll be back soon. And don't touch my stuff." I turned and walked out of the building, not waiting for Larry.

"Aren't you going to introduce me to your pals?" Larry complained.

Uh. That would have been the polite thing to do. Now I looked stupid. My mother would have given me the evil eye if a new friend came over and I didn't introduce them. *There had to be another movie quote to cover up my blunder.* "Say hello to my little friend!" *Classic Scarface!* I hope he understood the reference.

Larry responded, "I see you like movie quotes, too. 'I am going to make you an offer you can't refuse.'" *Godfather! Nice!* We both laughed at that. He's really good.

I grabbed Larry's arm and marched him back up the stairs into the cabin. I pointed to the first guy on the left and continued until everyone was identified.

"That's Dudley, a genius in math; Nicky can only use sign language and reads lips, and Stephen is best known as a booger-eater. Howie is always fun to have around, but don't pick him to be on your team. He's a lousy athlete. Ernie is the fastest kid in camp. Malcolm is a loner by choice. Alec will follow you into battle. Walter has been, and will always be, the tallest kid in school. Theodore is so skinny that he gets lost in the crowd. This is our gang of misfits. Still want to join us?" I asked, before turning and heading out of the cabin, down the hill and along the winding paths around the camp.

When he arrived at the lakefront, Larry stopped me. "You know, you described everyone but yourself. How would someone describe you?"

Me? That seemed odd to ask. Can't he figure out who I am just by talking to me? I don't go around assuming stuff about myself. How would I know?

I shifted my weight from foot to foot. I was uncomfortable talking about myself. "Oh, me? I'm a strong, mighty mountain ant, full of energy and friend to all." I crossed my arms, feeling proud of my description.

I nudged Larry, "What about you? How would you describe yourself?" Dad always said turnabout was fair play. "You're being a little tight-lipped over there." Larry's eyebrows pulled together as if he was deciding what to reveal.

"I am an only child; my parents are in high government positions, so the only rule everyone must follow is no pictures of me. Let me repeat that. No pictures of me! I know I am much bigger than all of you. I am strong, but I am not a bully. I will help everyone who needs me. I love sports, and I am very competitive." His comments were accurate from a physical perspective. As far as his parents went, though, I'd have to respect his wishes.

"Max, you like quotes. Here's one of my favorites, 'If you can't outplay them, outwork them!'"

"Oh no," I sighed, chuckling, "Another person with inspirational quotes, just like my dad." Larry looked a little worried for a second that it didn't go over well. "Nah, you're all good. I'm just reminiscing on something you don't have to worry about. In the meantime, we're back at our cabin, your new wilderness home for the month."

For the next while, we put our stuff away on the almost clean shelves at the foot of our bunkbeds. Larry finished before I did and walked around, reading the carved names in the wood paneling above and below all the bunks.

"What do you say we go find our bunkmates? I might know where they are." He shrugged his shoulders, and we began walking toward the sports fields, smiling and chatting with old friends.

"You been to camp before?" I asked.

"Nah, parents always wanted me close by. Never really got the chance to be off on my own until recently," he responded.

A kindred spirit, someone my age who gets how smothering parents can be.

"Here's a building we didn't see before. It's the group activity hall. It's gross. It features shag carpeting, peeling paint, and ancient furniture that pokes your tush when you sit on it. As of last year, it's no longer used unless it's an emergency. Then it's playing card games, charades, and team building for the day."

I moved Larry along the path and pointed to the next moldy-old place he might want to use, the arts and crafts building.

"They still use this building?" Larry asked suspiciously.

"That's a fair statement. If I'm not mistaken, they did build or are building another place that doesn't resemble the Addam's Family home." My body shivered, remembering my last visit to that building. Something fell from the ceiling, and I was positive it was blood. After closer inspection, it was painted plaster from a repair they made during a rainstorm, and it fell right at my feet, freaking me the hell out.

"Oh my God! Dude, that sounds so bizarre. I would have run like hell and not looked back!" Larry said, flinging his arms out wildly.

One of those arms flung over my shoulder, "You're hilarious. What else do I need to see?"

It was fantastic meeting someone as cool as Larry. I think this would be my best summer yet at camp. I saw something I wanted to show him and took off on a sprint. I must have surprised him because I heard him holler, "Wait!"

When I went to look back, I accidentally caught my foot on a root and almost faceplanted, except I remembered an old trick and instead tucked and rolled down the hill. By the time I stopped rolling, I was in a pile of leaves and branches, slashed with all sorts of cuts and bruises.

I spit a leaf out of my mouth, "That smarts."

Larry rushed over and looked at me, worried. I stifled a laugh at the thought of how I must look at him and burst into laughter. His worried frown melted, and he laughed, too. I stood, brushed myself off, and proceeded to direct him to the destination I had literally stumbled on—the sports fields.

"Down there is where all the action is. If you want to be anyone here at camp, you'll make a name for yourself in that field." I stood there proudly with my hands on my hips, remembering how I'd embarrassed myself my first year by throwing a shoe while running a foot race, but the following year, I redeemed myself by winning the sack race in my age class.

"You sure you don't want to patch yourself up first? You took quite a tumble."

"Nah, it'll buff out." I chuckled, blowing off my pain. Unless my arm swung by a thread, I'd press on because I didn't want to miss all the fun around me.

"Glad you're able to laugh it off like that. Means you're doing just fine." Larry nodded and returned to the hill, "Well, if we're going, lead the way." And lead the way I did.

10

THE HAPPY HYENAS

LARRY

It's been a while since I've spent a night in a cabin, much less able to hear the sounds of crickets at night with how quiet it got. It didn't matter that I was sweating, but it made wearing pajamas much more uncomfortable. Long gone was my Posturepedic adjustable bed engulfed in climate-controlled serenity. I'd deal with cracking my neck each morning and back strain when I got up for the joy of spending time with my son. He liked me. I saw it in his eyes and how he used those movie quotes like I taught him. I was having the time of my life!

Breakfast in the cafeteria was quiet, and a lot of people were getting used to the camp lifestyle again before going down to it for the day. The group was rowdy last night, getting back to the cabin from the campfire party. Apparently, this was a yearly occurrence, though I thoroughly enjoyed the newness of that first day of my camping experience. However, Max seemed unhappy for a different reason: a face I'm all too familiar with.

"Max, are you okay? You seem lost in your head." I asked, trying to pry gently. He looked up, a little frazzled.

"What? Huh? Oh yeah, I'm doing fine. It's just that camp activities start today, and Greg's group likes to take this opportunity to wield their dominance in front of everyone. A show of force, if you will, to get the other campers in line." He sighed resignedly and shoved another bite of Lucky Charms into his face.

Show of force? That seemed excessive for a camp environment. Where were the staff people who were supposed to keep these bullies at bay? Max needed another way, and I would teach him that the bigger they are, the harder they fall.

"Wanna try and beat them at their own game?" I asked, genuinely grinning at Max. He looked at me wide-eyed.

"What are you, insane? Right off the bat? We'll have to deal with their bullshit the whole rest of the month if we do what you're suggesting. Even if we do beat them, which is highly unlikely, we'll have a target on our back."

"Regardless, what is the first activity today?" I pressed on, not acknowledging Max's trepidation.

"Football. We have to pick teams from kids in our same age group; that's only two cabins of guys. Greg will force his way to be a captain of one of the teams...and we don't have many strong options on our side." Max looked back to his food.

My cereal was mushy at this point, but I ate it without tasting it. My courage was one thing, but gathering the courage of others to be bold enough to face down the enemy they saw was a whole other story. As a peer, I was an equal and, therefore, would have the kind of influence Max would listen to. Done with breakfast, I stood up, looked at Max, sharing a devilish grin, and marched down to the sports fields to stretch. I was amped up and getting ready for battle. This would be the first of many, and losing wasn't an option. I could settle on a stalemate, but I'd rather push them off balance and put them on the defensive. Every war needed a leader, and if Max needed a solid example to pick himself up, then I'd show him how it was done.

It wasn't long until both cabins arrived at the field. One cabin was meek and unsure, and the other formidable. My cabin was a sad state of affairs, but with a plan and a lot of confidence, they could leave this field with their heads held high.

"Well, well, at least one of you is trying. Not that it'll make a difference." Greg's smug expression made my stomach churn. I didn't give a crap that he was a child. I would make sure he went down.

"You sure? Getting into the groove does wonders for the mind. I'm surprised I didn't see you out here doing the same. Not afraid you're going to get stomped?" Did he want smack talk? I was more than happy to dish it back his way.

Max rushed to me frantically and whispered, "What are you doing? Why are you antagonizing him?"

I smiled back, confident and calm, "Relax, it's alright. Feel the rhythm." I knew he'd understand the reference.

Max's sigh of anguish and his muttering under his breath didn't leave me encouraged.

"Come on, Max. Feel the rhythm. Feel the rhyme. You have to know the movie "Cool Runnings?" I stood, not waiting any longer, and dragged him over to Greg.

"We're picking teams from both cabins, right?" I asked him, staring directly.

"That's the way we've always done it. Especially since it's the only way you nerds will *ever* have a chance." He sneered, drunk on his past victories.

"Captains, then. I assume you'll be one, and I will be the other.

"Max, you're my first pick." I looked at him and nodded, "You'll also be my co-captain." Max's eyes went wide. His look of bewilderment was priceless. He had no idea where that came from, and I swear his jaw dropped in surprise.

Greg laughed, "That small-ass kid? What can he do better than anyone from my cabin? Speaking of which,

Ira, get over here." Ira rushed over to Greg, displaying how manly they were by jumping in the air to chest bump.

This team was so cliché. Meatheads who didn't think for themselves, who never thought they were weak, or it was okay to show their vulnerability. It was pathetic. God forbid anyone tried to insinuate that they were weak since would send them off the deep end. Unfortunately, when they're shown to be weak, they lose all sense of purpose or fly into a wild rage. They had no idea this kind of bandwagoning would be their demise. Max slid next to me, excited and focused.

"It's our pick, so take Kirk, the heaviest, toughest bully out here." Max pointed to a big lug with a square head.

I chuckled, "Why are we set on convention? They'll never see it as a win unless we win with our strength."

"When did you become a psychologist?" Max jabbed. "As your co-captain, I'm saying that if you pick how I think you're going to pick, there's only one choice. . .

"We take Theodore," I said triumphantly. Grenade launched. Pin pulled.

"Who...I mean...what...I mean, why? Larry, are you totally off your rocker?!"

Max yelled, stomping around in a circle. "Do you not understand football? Do you not understand that we need muscle, weight, blocking, hitting, and tackling!"

Greg laughed at his temper tantrum. "Obviously, your teammates know you suck at being a captain.

This is going to be easy pickings." Greg's face showed feelings of overconfidence as he beckoned Kirk to his side. Max facepalmed his head. I hoped I didn't make the wrong decision.

"Smooth call, Larry, smooth call," Max said sarcastically. I pursed my lips and shook my head. He knew what I was about, so why not just lay it out plainly?

"Why don't we just do cabin vs. cabin?" I proposed. Greg looked at me, shocked at first, like the cat who ate the canary. I was no canary and wouldn't let my new friends get eaten alive by that crooked cat.

"Listen, guys. All we have to do is sit down and make a solid plan that utilizes excellent strategy and is not full-on brawn. We are so much smarter than them. That's how all the good generals won their wars: that and unwavering determination.

Greg looked on as my cabin turned their backs to him. Max whisper-yelled, "You'd better have a goddamn plan. But in the meantime, I think I have some ideas. If we're going to indulge in your insanity, I will indulge mine."

"All right, punks, you'll have four days to practice, and then we'll meet on the field. That's all the mercy you're getting. There will be two touchdowns to win the game. Fast, brutal, clean." Greg says, cracking his knuckles.

Max interjected, "A moment, if you will, just to help us understand the whole game and some extra rules that I think will help make the game more fun for everyone." Greg looked peeved but let Max continue to speak, "One touchdown must be by a pass into the endzone, and a run must make the other. And lastly, the same player cannot score both touchdowns."

Greg thought momentarily, as his face twisted into a devilish smile, "All right, kid, it's a deal. My team, The Warriors, agreed to those rules. The winner gets to decide a punishment for the losers."

I blurted out, "Our team's name will be The Happy Hyenas." Max looked at me like I was some weirdo. Greg chuckled.

"With a name like that, maybe you should go back with the little leagues, Pit-iful." He laughed, insulting us while he walked back to his cronies. Max grabbed me by the shirt.

"The Happy Hyenas? Really? Why?"

"Well, I know you don't like my inspirational quotes, so I went with fun vicious animal." Max rolled his eyes and sighed.

"Fine. I'll allow you to say it just this once." He said, words dripping in sarcasm.

"We're a group of fun guys, right?" Max nodded. "If you know anything about hyenas, you'd know they are vicious scavengers and run in a pack. They work together to surround their prey, and everyone benefits from that philosophy. Does the name make sense now?"

Max scratched his head and walked in a circle, processing what I told him.

"So, if I'm getting this right, we need to work together to build our confidence, and that's the way to win?" His look was quizzical, but he was starting to understand my logic.

I solidified his thinking: "It's like that gold-medal Olympic gymnast Mary Lou Retton said, 'Rather than focusing on the obstacle in your path, focus on the bridge over the obstacle.' This is what I want from us guys. It's not the physical strength that would defeat us, but the lack of mental strength to win this game that would put us under." Max sighed and gave a soft smile, looking over to his cabinmates for a moment before looking back at me.

"I get it now. I'm cool with the name." Max conceded as he pressed his fist to me, and I reciprocated.

"Let's make it happen."

11

WAR

LARRY

T raining for a battle against people who would normally be able to crush you without a second thought took cunning and cardio. On the one hand, the skills necessary to develop our bodies and team coordination weren't a luxury we had. On the other hand, the game was simple. We just needed to find a way to outsmart Greg's team and beat them at their own game.

The following day, our team hustled through breakfast so that we could practice and devise a game plan that would ensure a win. As captain, the first order of business would be increased stamina.

We all lined up on the twenty-five-yard line and ran sprints, led by me, to improve our cardio. Keeping up with the other team would be half the battle.

Dudley barely made it over the finish line. Alex and Malcolm looked like they were joined at the hip as if they were in a potato sack race. But Max and Ernie showed me their quickness. The others filed in slowly afterward, with varying efforts on the sprints.

"You two are pretty fast. Max was right about you." I nodded to Ernie. "You were pretty speedy, too, Max. One of the best we have for our team." Max glowed in my praise.

Max commented, "That's just Ernie and me, though. The rest of our team is an embarrassment. We're gonna get smoked out there."

"So? Now we know who our runners are and can find the others in the correct position for their skill level.

I grabbed Max and Ernie to the side. "I need you two on defense—sometimes." Max looked like his mind short-circuited for a moment.

"Excuse me?" Max stuttered. "Are...are you kidding me? Defense?"

"You expect me, the eighty-five-pound mighty ant, to haul through their terrifying offense. And get to Greg?" Ernie sarcastically quipped as well.

"Hear me out," I said quickly to reassure the two.

"Greg will be their quarterback. This we know for a fact." They nervously nodded. "He will be looking to plow through as much opposition as possible. Placing you two on defense will make you invisible to him.

"So, we're offense as well?" Ernie questioned, and I nodded.

"I will be the quarterback that can at least stalemate Greg. When we run right or left, one of you, depending on the side, will grab onto the bottom of my shirt and hug the out-of-bounds line while we run down the line together. Think of it as water skiing, and you're the skier. You're the skiers, and I'm the boat. They may try and take a bite at you, but we're playing a strategic game, not an entirely perfect one."

A couple more affirmative nods helped me know that I could continue.

"Max, your new rules are brilliant. By creating two different scoring methods, we might have a chance at succeeding with a well-planned attack. They'll keep us in the game and give us ways to throw them off guard, at least for the first touchdown and partially for the second. Greg will have to pass or receive at least one of the times he wants to make a touchdown. We'll need to press hard for the second one. That's where my next plan comes into action."

I waved the rest of the team over and explained what each man had to do. They weren't suited to blocking, hitting, or tackling, but they were kids well-suited to child-like endurance and acting like fools. This would be a great distraction. The noise would disorient, the movement would confuse, and general slapstick antics would become obstacles for our opponents. My plan was more like a shell game, shuffling the shells and providing distractions to bring us victory—*whatever it took to make my son a winner!*

I broke the team into small groups to hash out specific ball handling and blocking skills. Apparently, the guys didn't want Stephen touching the ball at all. I guess picking your boogers, eating them, and then touching the ball was gross. And I vehemently agreed. Max looked relieved when I put Stephen as a linesman.

Howie could throw high for sure, but his distance was severely lacking. Max had inherited my genetics of smaller hands, so he's unable to get a good grip on the ball. Walter, though, Walter surprised everyone. I whistled to hike the ball to him, and he launched the ball forty-five yards down the field in a perfectly accurate spiral. *Finally! A kid with an arm.* This guy would make the plays I called more consistent. I looked at Max encouragingly, hoping he understood that 'we're finding gems in this pile of coal.' He rolled his eyes knowingly and looked back to the team.

I huddled the guys after several plays and was pleased with their performance in the positions I'd assigned them.

"All right, now we need to see who can catch the ball," I called out. Nerves ran rampant throughout the group. I knew that if they treated the ball like molten lava, they'd never catch it. These guys needed the right mindset to do well, and we weren't leaving this field until they did.

"Larry, I know you said this is for eventualities, but you really should be the one to catch the winning pass in the endzone," Max said.

"Yes, I know, I know, but I genuinely believe that Greg will be expecting that and will sic everyone on me as soon as he catches wind of us trying to go for that play. So, let's spice it up a bit and give it a little razzle-dazzle. I will be the decoy. After all, he wants me, the new kid ruining his life. You, Max, my friend, will be the one to catch the touchdown pass, and I'll tell you how to do it. First, you need to pull out your shirt like this." I took the bottom of my shirt and stretched it out in front of me. Max looked at me weirdly again.

"Why?" he asked.

"We saw that your hands are small, no offense, so catching the ball with consistency will be a problem. However, no one said you can't use your shirt. Fair is fair." I grinned, to which he nodded, rolling his eyes. "Grab your shirt and hold it with both hands at the bottom, making it look like a basket. All you need to do now is learn how to get in position for that to work. And we had a few days to practice getting it right consistently."

"All right, well, on top of everything else, I guess I've got my homework." Max snarked, "It does sound like a fun idea, though. It'll be hilarious to see the look on Greg's face when we pull it off."

"Damn right," I said.

Three days of practicing flew by quickly, leaving everyone in a better place than they were before. It didn't matter that we missed all our electives; we were in it to win. I begged our counselor to let us stay on the football field instead of playing Capture the Flag. We were all willing to make the sacrifice if we could win just one game against Greg's Team.

As for Greg's cabin, I got some intel from overhearing a conversation at lunch yesterday. Per usual, they were chilling and enjoying summer camp their way, which consisted of taunting people and skipping required camp activities to goof off like they owned the place. They didn't seem worried, which was exactly how we wanted them: complacent, distracted, and overall, unprepared.

We arrived at the football field the morning of our game and continued training until Greg's cabin arrived just before ten. These guys might be the Titans they are, but we had the actual planning, training, and mindset to beat them. It was time to put that to the test.

The rest of the campers slowly filed onto bleachers to watch the game. This game was an annual camp event, and several cabins made signs reading, "Be A Champion!" or "Hold That Line!" There were several more specific to our team names, but I focused on keeping my attention in a huddle and not looking around to get distracted.

"All right, gentlemen, it's coin toss time." Sid, the camp director, said, pulling out a quarter from his pocket, "Heads, the Hyena's kick-off, tails Warrior's kicks off."

"Fine by me," Max said, standing shoulder-to-shoulder with his teammates. Sid flipped the coin, caught it, and slammed it on the back of his other hand. "It's...heads," he said. *It was too early for a Hail Mary play, but we were ready to tear these guys apart.*

"Awesome! Team Warriors for offense first." Greg growled his approval and fist-pumped the air. "You guys are toast."

The two teams lined up, preparing for the kickoff. Greg was the quarterback, as expected, which weaved into the formations and strategies we planned. They get the first offensive, but we have a laundry list of counter-offensives to stop them in their tracks. I lined up over the center, and, of course, I got the giant, Kirk, eyeballing me. Did the biggest guy on their team think he would waste me? Not a chance. *At least, I hoped so.* I whispered to Max and Nicky to get on either side of me so they could back me up in case this plan was a dud. They nodded and prepared for the hike.

Greg called out just then, "Hike!" Immediately, my legs burst forward, blasting through Kirk and tackling Greg to the ground. I reached down and grabbed his shirt with one hand and pointed to mine with the other while I stared directly into his eyes and yelled in his face.

"That's why they call me Pitbull. Sit your ass down!"

Max and my team were in shock as their stunned expressions of what happened crossed their faces. I released the grip on Greg's shirt, returning him to the grass. He looked shell-shocked but managed to slowly get to his feet and reposition himself back to the line of scrimmage. Shaken, I chuckled to myself. That ought to put fear into his head.

Greg whispered right and left to his teammates, jutting his jaw towards me, Max, and Nicky.

I warned my guys. "He's going to try and put pressure on me. He's scared of me now, so he doesn't want to take chances," I said to them. Max and Nicky nodded. "We're countering with a blitz. Sack this hack. It's time to throw him off his game for good."

The next play was ready to begin, and the crowd got quiet. No one expected the first play to land Greg on his butt. Even if he won this game, that play would live in infamy.

"Hike!" Greg called out, maneuvering himself backward to receive the ball. This time, both Kirk and Ira were flanking me. Even if I could make it to Greg, he would have time to make his play. I knew what I had to do and pressed into the pile of bodies trying to knock me down.

"Gotcha," I mumbled smugly. A thud sounded behind the wall of guys in front of me. I finished bulldozing through Kirk and Ira to see an incredible sight. Max and Nicky were on the ground, pinning Greg to the turf as the ball rolled out of his hands. The sack worked! My plan worked.

Greg uttered swear words under his breath as Max and Nicky got up and gave each other a high-five. She made a sign to Max, and Max sloppily tried to do one back. I'd recently discovered that Nicky liked being referred to as a girl. She didn't dare to tell her parents yet, and that's how she was placed in a boy's cabin. Girl or boy, this kid had plenty of talent for sports, and that's all any of us cared about. The irony is that if Greg knew a girl had taken him down, he would have been demoralized.

Yesterday, I pulled up a video of a pack of hyenas out on the prowl on the camp computer so the guys could get a feel for how they worked together. After they tackled Greg, the team whooped and hollered, making screeching sounds just like the sound byte of those hyenas. It was terrifying. My son and his team were starting to feel the rhythm I mentioned when I first met them, and that was only the beginning. Phase two of our diabolical plot was just getting started.

"Nice one, Max." I patted his back as he ran by me down the length of our teammates.

"You too, Larry. You really are a pit bull. How in the hell did you break through between Kirk and Ira like that?"

"That's the power of the Pitbull, baby!" I pointed to my shirt, smiling.

Our first battle may have been a victory, but Greg got up and started yelling at his team, throwing out insults about their plays and screaming desperate cries for people to be in their positions. It was quite a tantrum. Unfortunately, he wasn't the only one pissed off, and that was a perfect reason to tighten up our plans.

"Timeout!" I yelled to Sid, hovering over the sidelines. Greg rolled his eyes and gathered his team into a huddle.

"Listen, guys. We're doing good. Keep it up. They will be gunning for us, so keep your eyes open and be ready for anything," I implored the team.

"Hey, Larry. You keep doing you, too. You're a serious tank and a half." Max said, grinning at me. *I'd missed that smile.* He hadn't given one to me since before his bar mitzvah six months ago. There was *nachas* in my heart, and it only made me all the more motivated to keep that smile alive.

"It's not just me, Max. We play as a team and ride or die as a team." I said confidently. The group nodded, and our huddle broke.

It was third down, and we needed to break through their fortified line again. With his not-so-big-brain,

Greg put his big guys on the outside positions and his weaker players in front of me. It appeared he decided to take a play out of my book, but he didn't realize that he was sacrificing his players as I clobbered each one when I pushed through the center. I looked at Darius, their center, who was right before me. He was as nervous as a deer in headlights and wasn't doing anything to hide it.

"I'm not going to hurt you. But if you're not ready for this, lean to your right. I'll push you down, and they'll think you stood up to me. Sounds good?" He gave a subtle nod to me, steeling himself. I may be a sweet guy off the field, but I'm no one's doormat during competition. Eat or be eaten, and I was hungry.

"Uh, thanks, man." He gulped down his relief.

Greg called up the play and ran to the left as I brushed past Darius, pushing him down safely. This small mercy only gave Greg more time to enact his plans.

Spiraling a beautiful pass to Alfonso, who was open as he charged down the field, rushed into the endzone, and scored. The Warriors were in the lead, and Greg made no motion to deny his elation.

"YES! That's how it's done, boys!" He grinned with spite and excitement. After he high-fived his team, he strutted over to grab me by the shirt and bore holes into my head. "You think you're winning just because you got one good play? This is war, Pitbull. Our team is going to win, and you and your high horse can drop dead. Don't feel bad. The punishment I have in mind for you will have your team eating crow the rest of the summer." His spit hit my jersey as he spouted off full of himself.

"You're right about one thing, Greg. This is war. And you haven't even seen anything yet. Not in the slightest.

12

ON ITS HEAD

LARRY

M ax and I called the team over again between the plays to collect our bearings and remind them of the strategies we planned over these days. My team needed fortification, and this was where my leadership skills came into play.

"Listen up. I'm the quarterback for our offense. Max, stay to my left—Ernie, to my right, like waterskiing. Everyone else, take your positions." I looked at each player and gave them no option but to comply with my commands.

The guys hustled into position, and I bent low to receive the ball. I looked left and then right, determining whether there were any changes in the Warriors' formation. *None! Thank God.*

I waited moments until I heard that magical word, "Hike!" and Ernie latched onto my shirt. We booked it down the sidelines as fast as possible with an opponent on our heels.

The other team was baffled, trying to figure out what the hell we were doing. They wanted to stop us, but Ernie lost his grip on my shirt, and the play was over before we knew it. We strode out of bounds as the whistle blew, glad we got our first down. I'll take that any day of the week.

I patted Max on the back as we got back into formation. "Get ready," I said as I nodded over to him.

"Get ready for what?" Max said, a little nervous.

"Wake up and focus. You're going to need to run like hell." His face went white, and he slapped himself with both hands. He'd better hurry if he tried to get in the game; the snap was about to begin.

Numbers were called out, and the hike began anew. I ran left down the sideline, but Max wasn't there to grab hold of me, and three defensemen clobbered me into the dust. I called the group back for a huddle and stared down at Max.

"Where were you? We've practiced this over and over again," I said, annoyed.

Max broke out in a gruff laugh. "What we have here is a failure to communicate. You want me, small and easily crushable Max to grab onto the bottom of your shirt, flop around behind you like an innertube attached to a speedboat, and survive? Did I mention another speedboat coming at full speed, ready to pulverize me with his bare hands? That's what you're looking for?"

Holy shit! That was precisely what I wanted him to do, though forgetting about Max's health and well-being if it didn't work out.

He continued near hysterical. "Because that looked terrifying when Ernie did it. You said you'd be the bait for the sharks, but it's more like me being their prey."

Between the movie quote and the argument, I could see where Max was coming from. My vision was clear and logical, except I didn't have a issue—Max and his friends did. I couldn't fully assuage his fears, but I begged him for a leap of faith.

I pressed my hands together in front of me and begged him to listen. "Trust me, Max. Have confidence that this will work. If it doesn't, you own my ass for the rest of the camping session. Deal?"

"All right, you have a deal." Max sighed and began mumbling the Mourner's Prayer for the dead. I chuckled at the dramatic repose as he bowed his head, pivoted in three directions, and took one step backward, letting God in his space. At least he learned something from his bar mitzvah.

Sid called us back to play, and I roared to my team. "Be the hyena. Be a pack. We've got this!"

Play began again, and Max, as promised, worked the plan. I felt the tug on the back of my shirt, along with him screaming bloody murder as we ran for our lives.

The endzone was near when the pressure increased on my shirt, causing it to tear. *Crap!* Max hit the dirt, and I was tackled shy of a touchdown. I looked back to see the damage that down caused. Max was lying on the ground with the ball in one arm, and in the other, held by a pinching grip, was a big piece of fabric from the bottom of my shirt.

"I didn't let go," Max mumbled with his mouth eating the turf. "Your shirt failed me, though. I'm keeping it, 'cuz I'm never going to forget this play for the rest of my life!"

"Fair enough," I said as I reached out to pull Max to his feet, enjoying the shit-eating grin he made when he grabbed my hand.

Once the ball was hiked, we had two more downs to achieve our goal. This was our do-or-die moment, and we needed to keep our momentum. As we blocked the enemy team from capturing the ball, Ernie blitzed past, raced into the endzone, and did the most awkward endzone dance I'd ever seen. *Who's laughing now, Greg?*

"How is the war going, Greg?" I knew I was goading him, but I couldn't resist. My guys felt victory for once in their lives and would do anything to keep their spirits up.

"You haven't won yet, you little shit. It's two touchdowns to win. All this means it will be even more heartbreaking when you lose." Greg snapped back, annoyed.

I knew he'd bring the heat on his next play, and by the apparent gestures and red-faced contortions on his face, it wouldn't be pretty.

Paradoxically, the cheers around Ernie were deafening. Shy of one section, campers were dancing in their seats. It didn't matter that everyone wasn't behind us. We knew Greg had his cheerleaders. For once, though, most campers were backing us, and we didn't want to disappoint them.

Greg started the next play, and I could see that everyone saw him as a monstrous force. He moved with short passes, quick runs, and breakaways. He commanded his team to the ten-yard line, showing how much of a beast he was. We couldn't get sloppy in our confidence. He wasn't going to let us. I brought the group back into a huddle.

"We need the ball back. We can't let them score again." I ran my hand over my face, brushing my hair and the sweat off. "Here's the plan for our defense. I'll rush through the middle, disrupting their line, and Max, Ernie, you two need to swarm Greg like bees. The rest of you need to distract the other players. I need Max and Ernie to rip the ball from Greg while he's not focused on his hands to get him to fumble. Once you get that ball, start hauling it down the field." The team looked nervous but was willing to try.

Greg wasn't stupid. He was just an idiot. He saw what we were up to and finally put his heaviest hitters back in front of me to keep me from interfering. It was a bold choice that I would use to ruin his formation. I steamrolled through three guys before I watched our whole team swarm like a pack of hyenas attacking their prey. I looked to the side in time to see Max and Ernie sandwich Greg as they met in the middle, causing him to fumble. With his quick reflexes, Max made the decision and went for it. He covered the ball and rolled into it like a cocoon, protecting the pig-skinned ball with his body until he was lying on the ground in the fetal position, not even realizing what he had done.

I called to him as I rushed over. "Max, Max. We did it!" He wouldn't let anyone near the ball to the point he looked like a pill bug.

"It's our ball, the plan worked." I tried again. No response.

I shook him before he realized he had the ball and the play had concluded.

"Oh...oh my god, it worked." His eyes stared into space with an incredulous gasp. He stood slowly, trying to comprehend what just happened.

"Come on, buddy, let's close it out." I dusted off his back as we walked back to the bench. The crowd was going wild as if we'd just returned from war. I have to say, it was impressive to have his peers' support.

Everyone was hot and tired as the midday sun reached its zenith. Bugs zinged by my ears, giving me the heebie-jeebies, and flies attacked Ernie, who needed to learn to wear deodorant. Our team chugged gallons of water, trying our best to refresh ourselves, but the reality was no one was getting any rest until we kicked Greg's team's ass.

"Why the hell aren't you guys protecting me? Do you want them to win? Do you want to live in shame for the rest of the summer? You guys suck!" Greg threw his hands in the air, making any of Max's tantrums look like a kick in the dirt.

Max moved closer and asked, "You still think we can win? I know we've made it to this point, but we've got ninety yards to go."

I smiled, "Of course. I even think you'll be the one to score the winning touchdown. Remember the thing we practiced? It'll be time soon." Max nodded and remembered the shirt basket plan. I could see the whole thing playing out in his eyes. He was in the zone. Locked in and ready to be let out of the gate. "For now, though, rest. You will need all your strength to make that play successful."

"Right. Give them hell out there." He called over to me as I headed back to the field. I supposed he believed we could win this game, and if he genuinely believed it, so did I.

The next set of plays was quick and straightforward, utilizing each player within our team to our advantage. Our final strategy was to vary the runner. They'd never know who to mark, and chaos would ensue. It was our time to conquer the field. First, Howie made ten yards. Then, Malcolm made fifteen.

Greg outwardly showed signs of distress and yelled wildly, "STOP THEM!"

Stephen added another five yards, and Dudley took five as well. Nicky owned the defenders, and Alec delivered as well. We agonized down the field, but now we were in range for Walter and his insane arm to wrap up this battle with his gun-show arm. This was our moment.

"Timeout! Water break!" Greg called out. Both our teams returned to our benches to prepare for the next play.

"All right, Walter, you're going to be the new quarterback. We're doing the pass you've been practicing." Walter nodded, ready to do what was needed.

"I'll run down the left sideline and draw their attention. They know that I'm athletic and have a good chance of being the one to make the final play, so I'll need to be a decoy. Max, stay quiet and rush down to the endzone on the right sideline, shirt untucked for the maneuver."

"If you're so confident in your athleticism, why aren't you the one pulling off the catch? Why do I have to do it?" Max said, seemingly wavering in his faith in the play.

"Because you've told me about your experience with Greg, he knows your hand size. He already has a bias that you won't be able to catch the ball. And most of all, he wants blood from me after everything so far." I said calmly, trying to keep him from panicking. He took a deep breath.

"Ok. Let's do this." Max sighed.

The play began.

Walter looked at me as I bolted down the left side of the field, screaming to get his attention seemingly. I waited momentarily and then quickly turned towards Max, who was sneaking fast down to the endzone on the right.

Walter breathed in slowly and threw the ball like a laser. There is a moment in every sports game where the air leaves the field and time moves in slow motion. No one moves or breathes when moments of tension, pure adrenaline, and great expectations become reality. I savored this moment as Walter launched a perfect forty-yard spiral toward Max in the endzone. I wished I could fully admire its beauty if I weren't running for my life. What I could see, however, was Max untucking his shirt and making the basket with the bottom of it and the ball landing perfectly center in the basket. The crowd jumped from their seats in jubilation right before a sickening gasp. The ball bounced from impact, wobbling from the shirt basket as Max fell back into the endzone. Like a prayer coming from heaven, Max grabbed the ball and brought it to his chest, snuggling it tightly as he landed on the ground. The time continuum started again, and the cumulative roar of the crowd was a moment I'd never forget. It was a Hall of Fame moment I'll cherish forever.

Max laughed maniacally as he sat up, realizing what was in his hands—the ball. There was magic in his eyes as he began to understand what victory felt like. He jumped to his feet and leaped into the air, "I DID IT! We won!"

The crowd roared wildly as Max was swarmed by his teammates. I stood to the side, letting Max soak up his well-deserved glory. This was my father's wish coming true—my wish. This was the turning point in our relationship: Max got to lead the charge, and I *kvelled* in the shadows. This wondrous feeling of victory, pride, and friendship would make our relationship more profound and meaningful.

The realization that I was the one who needed to step aside and let Max shine on his own gutted me. I had been the real problem, not my son. True, he needed confidence but he needed to find it within. Once he had it, he took off like a rocket and made things happen. How could I have missed this? This slight shift in perspective seemed more like a chasm that spanned time and space. This was more than a father's wish. It was my son's wish, too. *It will be hell to let go of it when the month is over, but at least I have this in my heart right now.*

The group's cheers ring out through the camp: "HAPPY HYENAS! HAPPY HYENAS! HAPPY HYENAS!"

Max looked like he was having the time of his life right now. I walked over to join him but saw Greg coming over first.

"All right, nerds, fine. You beat us. Fair is fair. What's your punishment for us?" Greg said, annoyed. Max looked over with the smuggest look I had ever seen from him and said, "We'll let you know later. Larry and I need to...marinate on this a bit. After all, you need time to deal with this heartbreaking loss, right?" He said, dripping with sarcasm. Max hustled back to his friends, enjoying the victory. Greg spun around and stormed off, bumping into me hard as he stomped away. No words, just fury. This will haunt him for the rest of his life. He wouldn't want it to happen again. Unfortunately, this would be one of many losses for him throughout his athletic career. After all, this was war. Max and I wouldn't give another opportunity to rub our faces in the dust. Our cabin was not going to let him win.

*kvelled – Yiddish for bursting with pride

13

THE TASTE OF VICTORY

LARRY

The team was ecstatic as we headed to the mess hall for lunch. The camp was buzzing, rehashing the game and our unlikely victory. It was a true underdog story they'll be talking about for years to come. However, I can only guess that if we lose next time, it will just be called a fluke. Who cared? WE WON!

This was our finest hour, at least for now. Lunch felt more like a feast than the usual grub days prior. Trays of mac-and-cheese, pasta, and pizza were served on stone circles. The head chef, Duke, even made his unique concoction, "Frog Juice." It was like bug juice but made with pink lemonade, fruit punch, and a secret ingredient he wouldn't share. We were royalty—for now, and life was good.

I saw Max eyeing the big container of sickeningly sweet punch, a glint of devilish thoughts behind his eyes. I knew that look. I knew his mischievous intention because he stole it from me. I hoped he knew what he was doing.

"Max, you're up to something. Anything you want to share?" I grabbed a couple of slices of pizza and a heaping pile of mac-and-cheese, waiting for him to say what I already knew.

"Yeah...I'm thinking it's punishment time." There was a cunning in his voice, the feeling of victory seeping into every word and revenge on every consonant.

"I think I have the perfect idea for a very fitting punishment. Greg and his cronies act like nasty bugs that ruin our days at camp, and I'm tired of it. Set your plate down, Larry. It's go-time."

"Yes, sir." I stood and saluted him, then gathered the remaining guys in our cabin.

Max stood resolute in his mission, finally finding the confidence to take charge. It was exhilarating to watch, and I couldn't imagine how this punishment would play out, but we all had his back.

"Greg, we have decided on your cabin's punishment."

"Well, speak up, I don't have all day to deal with your bullshit." He snarled, still looking at his food.

"You need to go to the camp storage building tomorrow and take out some cots and tents for camping. Have them outside the mess hall before dinner because your cabin will sleep under the stars in your team's jerseys." Max said, going over the punishment in detail.

"Really? That's all? Easy." Greg smirked and shook his head, "What was I worried about with a bug like you calling the shots?"

Max rolled his eyes and started walking off, whistling with a spring in his step.

Ernie piped up, "What's the real deal with what they're going to be doing? Cause I know that is not all their punishment will be," he sputtered out.

I signaled my friends over to the kitchen and the extra container of Frog Juice.

"Hey, Spencer, can we get a spray bottle?" Max asked Spencer, one of the chefs in charge around here.

"Sure, just remember to bring it back." He tossed one at Max, who caught it confidently and motioned for us to exit the kitchen.

Max gathered us into a huddle and delivered the nail in the Warrior coffin.

"It's a stealth operation." The group looked at him quizzically. "While Greg's cabin is at lunch tomorrow, we'll sneak into their cabin, spray this juice all over their jerseys, and wait for nature to take its course. They'll never know what hit them."

Walter interjected, "But tomorrow will be over ninety degrees, and this God-awful humidity will."

Realization hit him and the rest of the guys. "I wasn't kidding when I said nature would take its course. They'll be crawling out of their skins."

"You're a madman. A maniacal madman. Does that come from your mom's side of the family or your dad's?" I asked.

"Definitely my dad's side. He's a sick bastard." We laughed and pushed each other back to our seats, chowing down at our victor's meal.

"You're a lot like him in many ways, and others, not so much. In a good way, though." I smiled, realizing this was one of the first times in a long time that he'd spoken about me in a positive light. I held that feeling tightly to myself, glowing within. He meant what he said, and I'd take that to the bank.

The rest of the day came and went, filled with anticipation of what was on the horizon. After sharing all the details with the cabin the night before, no one said anything until we prepared to inflict our revenge the next day.

"Hey, Larry. Do you want to come with me and help set up the radio stuff for the camp today? Maybe put on a show just for kicks?" Max whispered conspiratorially. He looked jazzed up, donning a red bandana wrapped around his head like the kid from the Karate Kid movie. I didn't know what he was going on about, but I was all in if it meant we could hang out together.

"Sure. Just give me a second to get myself together. It's still early in the day, and I sound like I'd smoked a pack of cigarettes— if I had smoked cigarettes."

"All right, but make it quick," Max said as he sassed me. I put on a shirt, wincing, remembering the demise of my Pitbull shirt. I collected the water bottle, stuffed it into a cinch bag, and threw it over my back.

With light footsteps, we headed to the radio building next to the mess hall. As I entered, I looked around at all the equipment while Max beelined to set it up. He adjusted the microphone, pulled over a device I didn't recognize, checked some papers nearby, and then peered over the itinerary sheet. Max cleared his throat and fidgeted in his chair. It's apparent that he's done this before, and honestly, I'm surprised at the level of knowledge and understanding of the camp he had. He breathed in and then out, preparing himself just like we did in my big leather chair at home. After two rounds of breathing, he pressed a button on the device that signaled a red light near the door, illuminating the words: On Air.

"Good morning, campers!" An impeccable Robin Williams impersonation from *Good Morning Vietnam* burst from his tiny body. "Time to rise and shine, and let's have another great day at Camp Windy City. There are no big camp events today, but the older teen cabins are going on their annual canoe trip. Safety first, fellow campers. Have an awesome time. Don't you worry, younger campers, we haven't forgotten about you. Today, there is a great activity planned at the beach. Be sure to meet at the Flagpole immediately following breakfast to learn the details. In the meantime, let's let Mr. Blue Sky from E.L.O. get your blood pumping. From us to you, "get blown away" at Camp Windy City today."

Max plugged in his little MP3 player, and the music blared across the camp. I was so proud of him. Thoughts of what he could do with that voice whirled around my head. Minutes later, the song was over, and Max let go of the microphone, clicked a few buttons, and pulled out the input.

"That was cool, man." I grinned at him as he stood.

"Yeah, I learned how to do this two years ago, and I got permission this year to do it a couple of times throughout the camp session. It's honestly a little bit of a hobby I wish I could explore, but I doubt that I'd get much help from my dad. He's more interested in sports stuff, if you know what I mean." *Busted*. I would have never known had he not just told me. He's right. I didn't know. I suppose that's another thing I need to learn—how to listen better.

"Have you told him the kinds of things you like to do? I bet he doesn't know yet." I encouraged him to consider. "I think he'd understand if he knew you loved doing it."

"Maybe," he agreed. "I guess I could try when I go home, but he's always forcing me to do what he wants. It's exhausting."

I sighed, knowing exactly what he meant. "Do you like nature? I mean, there are some great trails you could hike around camp. Oh! What about mountain biking? It's a blast. You get to challenge yourself and see nature." I noticed myself rambling and forced myself to stop. Max laughed, giving me a shove.

"I'm not a bike rider. It's not my first choice of wheels. I like rollerblading. It's fast, fun, and dangerous, so you get that thrill factor. Thanks, Larry. I appreciate you listening." His lopsided grin hit me right in the heart.

"Admittedly, I haven't rollerbladed before, either. I'm an old-fashioned roller-skates kid, you know? More wheels, more stability, a little less danger of falling. I'm not a fan of eating dirt." I put my arms in front of me and wobbled to bring the point home.

"I get that, but maybe we can try blading later on. I think you'll like it. With your crazy stamina and physicality, you'd be great. Maybe we could see some FTBs while going blading?"

I stopped in my tracks, laughing. Dale must have brought it up to him before.

"What do you know about FTBs?" I queried.

"Not much yet, but wait a minute, do you even know what FTBs are?" Max gave me a curious look.

"Sure do, Full Titty Bra, it's common knowledge," I brushed it off, mainly because there weren't any other people who would know about the term besides Dale and me. *Shut it, Howard! Don't blow your cover.*

Most days at camp, we had structured activities, which were great, but I treasured free time when I could walk and talk with Max without being interrupted. Today was no exception. As we walked toward the sports fields, we rehashed our victory and what foods we ate. Today, I learned he hated hotdogs but loved steak. *He was a kid after his dad's heart.*

When we arrived at the tennis courts, we stopped short, noticing Greg practicing his serve. He was completely focused and didn't see us approaching. I felt a premonition coming on, and a shiver ran down my back. I may have been a good footballer, but fearing we might have another face-off on the tennis courts in the near future wasn't anything I was looking forward to. I looked over to see Max concerned.

"So, have you played tennis before?" I said. I knew *he* had. I paid hundreds of dollars every summer for lessons at my club.

"Yeah, I have. I think I'm pretty decent. Have you?" Given his talent, Max scratched the back of his head, not looking as confident as he should.

"A few times before. I even brought my racquet with me to camp. Speaking of which, have you been to a tennis camp before? Because I noticed your racquet is pretty high quality." Larry inquired.

"Yeah, apparently, it was super expensive. My dad wanted me to have the best one possible for a tennis camp I went to a few times when I was younger."

"I brought my own. It's a classic. Jimmy Connors used to use the same type, the T2000." I played dumb, though, feeling nostalgic. Max looked at me and stifled a laugh.

"Who the hell is Jimmy Connors? I've never heard of him." Max asked. *Quick— adjust, adjust, adjust!*

"He was this big-time tennis pro my dad and I used to watch. He got me all excited about sports, and I learned a lot of stuff about a lot of athletes. My grandfather said I was an 'enthusiast.' I like playing sports, but I also like studying the history and past players of the games."

"Huh. Neat." Max gestured to keep walking to the other side of the courts. *Another bullet dodged.*

We walked a little further while I debated, expounding on the book The Art of War by Sun Tzu. Max hated being "preached to," so I blurted out, "Know thy enemy."

As expected, he gave me a funny look.

I ushered Max back the way we came. "Go ahead to breakfast. I'll catch up soon. I'm going to watch Greg for a little while."

"That's cool. Just don't blame me when all the food is gone."

I marched to the top of the small bleachers next to the courts and sat down to study his game. Greg had a strong serve, forehand, impeccable footwork, and an overhead smash that could take off a person's head. He was formidable. Finding fault in his game was tough.

Without the experience and knowledge of the game I had acquired over decades, I wouldn't have even stood a chance against him.

After several minutes, his weaknesses began to show. He wasn't a net player. Shots that flew low or on his backhand side messed up his footwork, causing him to hesitate. Tucking that nugget of intel away, I rushed to breakfast, knowing Max was waiting.

14

SWEET REVENGE

MAX

This was it. Greg's cabin had their make-shift camp set up by the mess hall, and it was finally time to realize my pipe dream —revenge. I knew that revenge was not a good thing, but this...this would heal past wounds that tormented me from all my years as a camper here at Windy City. My plan was simple. First, we'd run to the jock's cabin during dinner. Then, we spray their jerseys with Frog Juice and return to the mess hall before being noticed. It was just that simple. No plot twists, shenanigans, or drama. Instead, Larry ran interference pissing off Greg to no end at his table in the cafeteria, giving us cover.

Ernie, Walter, Nicky, and I crept into Greg's cabin immediately following the dinner bell. It was obvious who washed their jersey after the game and who didn't. The smell was rotten, and we gagged, searching through their laundry. Like ghosts, we were in and out in less than five minutes. It was hilarious how we all looked left, then right, like an office chair swiveling from side to side. Thank God we didn't see anyone lurking about. Three of us walked into the mess hall while Walter ran behind the building, washing and returning the spray bottle to the kitchen.

"Sorry, we're late," we sat down with our trays at our cabin table. "We finally got that radio equipment to work. Loose wires. The bane of my existence." I projected it to the other tables around us in case anyone wondered why we were late.

Ours was a perfect crime. I smiled, devious thoughts roiling in my head for future punishments.

"Hey, kid!" Duke called out. "Congrats on the win yesterday. Sorry, I wasn't able to tell you sooner. I was a bit busy trying to get things ready for lunch after the whole event. Sid organized a video for the rest of us who couldn't make it. I'll watch it later tonight. You're a hell of a player, that's for sure." My chest swelled with pride.

"Thanks, man, I've been trying hard. It's nice to get a win finally. Making that winning touchdown felt fantastic. By the way, I dropped that thing I borrowed yesterday back in the kitchen earlier. Thanks for the loan." Duke came over and patted me heavily on the back.

"Shiiit, you are getting into trouble, kid?"

"Nah, cleaning up a few things."

"If by 'cleaning up' you mean wreaking revenge, you do realize you're poking the bear, right?"

"Yeah, but if nothing else, I'll leave things better than when I found them." I cracked myself up.

"Good luck, kid, that's all I'm going to say. I'll leave a late-night snack in your cabin when you finish whatever you're *not* doing." Duke broke into laughter with me and walked out of the dining room.

"Oh, what were you two talking about?" Larry leaned over the table, curious.

"Dinner and a bedtime snack since we won big yesterday. Sloppy joes and more mac and cheese. He has chocolate pudding for dessert. He knows I'd like to take a bath in that stuff. His is sooo good."

Larry rubbed his belly, "The only thing better than chocolate pudding is lava cake with vanilla ice cream. The best!"

The rest of the day went quickly. We went to the activities we signed up for at the beginning of the week. We did that every Saturday so the counselors and staff could prepare for the following week. Today, I coaxed Sid to change my schedule. Additionally, I had to convince Larry to detach from me so I could prepare for tonight.

I slung my arm over Larry's shoulder, or what I could reach of his shoulder.

"Hey, Larry. Do me a favor and spy on Greg at the tennis courts to see if you can gather new intel on his game. Something tells me we will battle again soon, and I want to be ready."

Rid of any interruptions, I ran to the broadcasting room and grabbed a microphone and amplifier. Sid allowed me to use the dining room stage after a lot of whining on my part. I was used to speaking behind a microphone in the comfort of a loft, but in front of a couple hundred campers was another story. I gathered myself quietly, remembered that weird breathing thing my dad harped on me about, and tried to use it to settle myself into a Zen state. Admittedly, it worked again. Of course, I'll never say that to my father. I'd never hear the end of it.

I finished my sound check and switched off the equipment in search of my elective group. I felt bad about blowing it off because I liked creative writing. The counselor was cool, and there was this girl, Elena. She had the sweetest smile. If I could get the courage to speak to her, I might have a chance to kiss her—or *next summer.*

I walked out to the beach, where everyone wrote in their notebooks. After asking the counselor for the assignment, I sat down with my notebook and began to describe boats, water, and the sky with the rest of the group. None of that seemed as interesting as locating Elena in the group. Sadly, she wasn't there. So much for creating an opportunity to talk with her—*or tomorrow.*

Later, in the mess hall, I mounted the stage lighting, tested sound equipment, and imagined the surprise punishment our team would announce. It was going to be epic! As I finished, the other campers stormed into the mess hall, and that was my cue to get myself focused. Speaking behind a microphone when no one was looking was very different than having two hundred kids staring you down like you were under a microscope.

I hated to admit that I needed my dad's breathing exercises, but I did. I walked to the back of the stage and faced the curtain to take several deep breaths. With each inhale and exhale, I visualized that balloon blowing across the room, settling into a peaceful place. It was surprising how much easier it was to return to that place of calm each time I went through the process. I noted that it was getting easier and faster to attain calm and turned to face my audience. I walked forward to the amplifier, flicked on the equipment, and stepped out of my comfort zone.

"Ladies and gentlemen, and that technicolor rainbow in between, how are we doing tonight?!" I called out from the stage. There was a wave of small cheers, jeers, and other mumblings as the other campers began to notice me. Some kids stopped talking, and others went back to their conversations.

I didn't wait for everyone to quiet down but kept going. "As you all know, The Happy Hyenas won this year's football game." The crowd roared, and I waited to continue.

"But you may not know that there was a bet made that the loser had to accept." The roars got bigger, and tingles burst out all along my spine.

I gestured out towards Greg's cabins' table. "As captain, Greg agreed that his team would spend a night under the stars. Sounds great, right?" Mumbles echoed throughout the room with shouts of 'What?' or 'Big deal.'

"No comfy beds, evening activity, or bedtime snacks tonight, fellas. Enjoy your night on the cots, and don't let the bed bugs bite. And don't forget to wear your game jersey!" I controlled my face to not give anything away, but I felt like another victory had been won. My cabin slapped each other on their backs and giggled like a bunch of girls.

I cleared my throat and pulled a three-by-five card from my pocket with this evening's announcements.

"In other news, we've got the ropes course at the end of the week for the older teen cabins, with the early teen cabins getting their swing, pun intended, the following week. The archery range is now open, and our younger campers will have their first crack at that tomorrow morning! In the event of rain, there will be a classic movie marathon in the Rec Building, and if it's sunny, practice for the camp Olympiad will begin after breakfast. See your counselor for more information. That's all for now. Have a great night!"

I hopped off the stage and smiled ear-to-ear as I caught up with my cabinmates. Unfortunately, Larry looked mortified.

"What's got you riled up, Larry?" I asked, concerned.

"Nothing, just thinking about something I forgot to do."

"Gotcha. Well, hopefully, it doesn't get you down," I consoled him.

"Listen, Captain Cryptic, try not to talk in circles. You'll make yourself dizzy." Larry cackled, and the rest of us joined in like a bunch of the happy hyenas we were.

Our evening activity was distracted by conversations about what was happening in Greg's small camp by the mess hall. When our counselor called "lights out," we agreed to sneak out to see if our evil plan had worked.

With flashlights stuffed in our waistbands and baseball caps swung backward on our heads, doing our best impression of the Goonies, we lined up single file and trekked through the trees as silently as we could until we found a spot close enough to listen to their conversations.

Greg announced he was hangry, followed by Kirk complaining about how itchy he was. They talked about feeling scratchy, and Ira moaned about the heat. Before I knew it, Nicky's army crawled to the front of their tent, unzipped the zipper halfway up, and scooted back in reverse.

Larry hissed, "What the hell, girl? Do you want us to get our butts kicked?"

I praised her, "So smart, Nicky. Why didn't I think to do that?"

There was a tap on my shoulder, and I thought we'd been caught, but it was only Duke. *Oh, crap!*

"Give it fifteen minutes. The whole tent will be filled with bugs. You kids are hilarious. Glad I'm not the one with a target on my back," and he walked away whistling softly.

It only took five minutes, and the tent erupted in a swarm. *BEST. NIGHT. EVER!*

Morning arrived, and all was quiet. The temperature and the bugs both dropped down to bearable levels. My cabin dragged their feet as we made for the mess hall, feeling accomplished. I did my best not to fuel the fire, but I'm a kid, and kids are kids.

"Did you see anyone coming out of the tent? That joke was so boss." My smugness wasn't hidden, and neither was Larry's reply.

"Who's the sucker now, right?" He softly punched me in the arm, and I pretended to fight him back.

We quietly munched on our breakfast as my mind second-guessed our prank. Larry looked over and smiled, followed by a nod for some reason. It was another reminder of Dad's *nachas* face, but that thought floated away quickly.

I stood to go over to the kitchen, needing to ask Duke a favor, when the "tent people" entered the building. They looked horrible. Bodies covered in scratch marks, itching rashes, and bug bites the size of ping pong balls. There were so many bug bites. *Yeah, remorse set in.* I drifted into the kitchen quickly, avoiding confrontations first thing in the morning. I mean, come on? They looked like zombies.

"Hey kid, what's up?" Duke cocked his head to the side, wondering what I needed.

"Can I ask a favor? I think I screwed up, and I might need to make sure that I don't get gutted right here and now."

"What'd I say, kid? The bear has been poked. I'll bail you out this time, but you must pay me back. It doesn't have to be this summer, but one day, when I knock on your door, the answer better be "yes." His ominous laugh was frightening.

"All right, Godfather, I will repay this debt when you ask." I shot back.

"So, what's this favor you want?"

"Can you let Greg's cabin into the cooler for thirty minutes to help them with their bites and to literally cool down? And could you make up a vat of baking soda and water so these guys have something to remedy the pain later?"

"Sure, that's fine," I nodded, backing out of the room.

I yelled over to Greg and his cabin, "Hey! Duke said you could go into the cooler to help calm your bug bites!" I stepped to the side and swung open the kitchen door, allowing the herd of wild animals to stampede through. Duke's laugh was loud at their lack of tact and overt desperation. I couldn't blame them. As funny as the punishment was, those bites would leave scars if not treated.

"Stop by the kitchen office on your way out. He has a box of baking soda to help settle down the bites." Grateful eyes beamed my way, and I had trouble looking back.

Duke yelled, "Don't touch anything in my cooler. Otherwise, you're paying for the next meal." Like that, clamoring stopped, and the lemmings slowed their roll. Duke closed the door and set a timer for thirty minutes. He laughed and looked over at me, hiding behind a rolling shelf.

"You poked a herd of wildebeest, not just a single bear, you crazy kid." My face flushed, sighing with relief, knowing I had somewhat repented. Larry warily poked his head into the kitchen.

"Hey, are you both okay?" He looked at Duke and me, who began prepping for the next meal.

"Yeah," I said, wiping my forehead. Duke lifted his hand in a knifed salute.

"What happened to all the revenge stuff? Letting them suffer would have been way better." Larry said, a little worried.

"It's still there. They will be feeling it into tomorrow, the next day, and the next day. You get it, right?"

I found a stool in the corner, dropped onto it, and continued. "I can't help but feel it was the right thing to do. We're all here to enjoy summer camp, even if things get too competitive. We're not here to inflict pain. We're here to have a fun rivalry."

"You realize that if he sets his mind on retaliating, we'll clean the latrines with toothbrushes." Larry moaned, and I followed suit.

Maybe he's right. Perhaps I made the wrong decision to spray those shirts. It didn't matter that I took the high road. It was too little, too late.

The timer went off, and Duke pulled open the cooler, freeing the now-chilled campers. They looked like the villain from Home Alone who got buried in the snow, shivering and annoyed. Greg looked over at me, taking a second for his gears to click since his mind slowed from the cold. He turned menacingly in my direction.

Larry ran for interference but stopped as Greg exuded an aura of controlled hysteria. I felt a cold shiver run down my spine as he approached me. My eyes went wide as he grabbed me by the top of my shirt and lifted me into the air until we were face to face.

"Listen here, you little shit," he said quietly, venom in every word. "The only reason you are alive right now is because you did us a favor. I respect that but know that this is your only freebie. However, you and four of your best players will be on the basketball courts tomorrow. We will rerun this challenge, whether you like it or not. If your pests don't show up, consider your life over. I will show you that you don't deserve to stand on the same field and make you grovel under my heel." So *dramatic*! It was too bad that I was focused on my great response or I would have been better prepared when he threw me into the refrigerator. I thumped to the ground, stunned and shaken up. He then turned to Larry. Murderous intent emanated from his eyes as if he dared to question his command. Greg gathered his crew and left the kitchen, kicking theoretical dust behind them.

Duke hissed out a slow whistle, "Goddamn, you are screwed, kid," and continued his prep work, shaking his head. Larry rushed over to me and helped me get to my feet. I was still shell-shocked, though. Despite my athletic ability, basketball was definitely not my game. I'm not tall and can barely hit the backboard from anywhere on the court. Was Duke right? If so, I was screwed. Larry, however, had that sparkle in his eye again that tells me he may have a way to help even things out.

15

FLOAT LIKE A BUTTERFLY

LARRY

Max, are you ok?" I asked, pulling him to his feet. That scene was terrifying. That teenager had me shaking in my boots. Whatever plan I was hatching, better be a winner, or I'd be carrying my kid home in a figurative casket.

"Yeah...I'm good. You'd better have a plan for the basketball game." He begged, his steepled hands tucked under his chin, and he was Jewish.

"I'm working on it. I have bits and pieces in my head, don't get me wrong, but I don't have a full plan yet." I put my arm behind his shoulder and started walking. "Let's walk and talk back to our table." He didn't resist, and Duke waved to us as we took our leave.

"Well?" Max asked me again.

"Well, first, we must pick our other three guys. Walter is an obvious pick for his height." I said, looking down at Max. "No offense."

Max nodded in agreement, laughing it off as much as he could. "None taken. I would have offered him up even if you didn't. We need all the advantages we can get. What do you think about Dudley? He's big, though a little clumsy, but he is good at analysis. That leaves us with one more space. I think Alec would be good. He listens well and is a good team player. What do you think?"

"Maybe—or Malcolm. After breakfast, we'll have to check their strengths and weaknesses." I said, thoughts still roiling about how we got dragged into another impossible situation. I released my arm around Max's shoulder and sat at our table.

Howie S. leaned over and whispered. "What the hell happened in there? Did Greg accept your olive branch of peace and let you off with a warning?" He said, mocking me. "Greg looked ready to rip someone's head off coming out of the kitchen."

"If I said I nearly died, would you believe me?" Max chuckled nervously.

"Holy shit, dude. Well, at least you're here." He leaned over the table again and slapped Max on the shoulder.

"We're not out of the woods yet, though," I sighed. "We're going to need to practice. At least, Max, Malcolm, Alec, Dudley, Walter, and myself." The guys called immediately, turning their heads in my direction.

"Huh?" They said, almost in unison. The dissonant chord of their voices was disconcerting.

"Yup. You are the chosen ones to beat Greg and his goons in the next challenge. If we don't go, we'll be labeled losers, at the least. If we lose, we'll probably be cleaning the latrines with toothbrushes and never be able to show our faces in public again." Max wailed. *Not on my watch!*

I felt terrible about Max spending his whole camp session protecting his dignity instead of having a carefree time. Hell, I was feeling bad for myself to have spent all this money, not to have him having the best time of his life! I suppose it wasn't all a loss. Max did win his first football game. He did feel the thrill of victory, but losing this next battle could be the agony of defeat. I needed a solid plan—now!

Again, I had to beg Sid to let us out of our electives to practice. I understood he wasn't happy about it but took it in stride, knowing we "little guys" needed redemption. He begrudgingly gave in after promises of never asking him again.

My team marched across the camp in silence, awaiting their new orders. I could tell they weren't happy about putting themselves on the line for a possible slaughter. Hell, I didn't want to either, but I wasn't leaving this camp with my kid feeling like a loser. We would devise a plan, practice as much as time would allow, and then, God help us, conquer again.

I stopped Max before we hit the break in the tree line. "Go ahead and stretch out, guys. We'll be right there."

"Max, I have something I want to try. Do you want to score more shots in basketball?" I asked. He gave me his signature sarcastic eye roll.

"Does a bear shit in the woods? Of course, I do, but I'm small. I don't have the height those beasts have or the strength to fend them off."

"Let's figure out what you can do to help your situation. I saw some ankle weights by the pool. Go now and find them. I'll be over in a minute to give you a routine."

"Roger, Roger," Max mumbled to himself, spewing another movie quote. Now, it was me who was rolling his eyes.

"Listen up, the rest of you. You're running sprints for the next fifteen minutes. Walter, use the timer on your watch and run from the baseline to the center line and back, then to the opposite baseline and back. Run those ten times, then get some water. Be back soon."

I arrived at the poolside gym and saw Max strapping on some ten-pound ankle weights.

"These will make my legs stronger and make me jump higher?" Max walked the length of the pool and turned around.

"They would, but you're going to wear them on your wrists only."

I ignored his consternation and strapped on a set of weights, gaining a look of disgust.

"What the hell, Larry? Weights on my wrists won't help me off the ground. Please explain before I wrap these around your neck and push you into the pool."

Like that would ever happen.

"It's simple, Max. The added weight will make your arms and legs work harder, so when they come off, every step and every free throw will be lighter and easier to make. Get it?"

He pondered a long while and then had a light bulb moment. "Oohh!" He dragged out. "Like gravity boots, right?"

"Exactly, but for your wrists. Take the damn weights off your ankles and put them on your wrists. End of conversation." I winked, dipping my head in his direction.

Max did a double take, then broke into peals of laughter.

"You sounded just like my father." *Oh shit.*

"You'll wear these weights day and night until the game. Understand? Shower with them. Sleep with them. They stay on until the game. Promise?" Max hung his head, surrendering to my orders.

I gave him a complete set of exercises and turned to leave the fenced area when I heard Max yell, "You're insane, but I'll trust you." Max swung his arms up and down, getting used to the extra weight. "You better hope this works because it's both of our asses if we lose."

I yelled back, "Like you said, trust me. This'll work." I *hoped*.

Our afternoon training made a few things evidently clear. While Alec was a loyal friend, he didn't possess the overall skillset we needed and was much happier acting as our team medic. Additionally, the cardio work we improved on in the football game was still strong, making Walter and Dudley our forwards. I was pleasantly surprised the team could run sprints far faster than expected. Lastly, Max honored his promise and kept every weight band on for the whole twenty-four hours since we began. However, there was a fair amount of whining as he pulled himself into the top of his bunk bed at the end of the day.

Another day dawned, and while the rest of our cabin went about their business after breakfast, our chosen team spent two hours learning and running plays. Our game was scheduled for what should have been free time, but again, there was no rest for the weary.

16

WEIGHTS OFF

LARRY

B oth teams met at center court, and Sid took his
place as referee.

"By the powers invested in me by the State of Illinois
and the mandate of Greg Wilson, today's basketball
game will *not* be a traditional match. The game will be
HORSE. I'll flip a coin to see who has the opening shot.
We begin in five minutes."

Our team gasped upon hearing about the game
change. I didn't blame them. It never occurred to me
that he wouldn't have a full-court game. It's time to
pivot.

Oh shit, all the plays we practiced are of no use. I
had so many plays drawn up, with me blocking out the
other team and allowing us to make some easy layups.
I was such a beast with rebounds, and no one would
come close as I swung my elbows to the right and

left; I looked like a human blender shredding anything that got in my way. When I played basketball with my brothers, though it was supposed to be basketball, it was more like tackle football. *There were no refs calling fouls!*

I huddled the guys up. "Max. The weights. When I nod to you, take them off."

"What?" Max broke his focus for a moment.

"You heard me. When I nod to you on the court, take the weights off and throw them to the side."

"All right, I guess," he said, confused. "I'm starting to get attached to them, though." He clapped his hands playfully.

The rest of the group bantered around half-heartedly, then faded away quickly. Our understanding that we could very well hang our heads in shame in the next hour weighed heavily on all of us. We padded over to our bench, the sun burning into asphalt, making heat auras burn into our vision.

Our game wasn't a secret for long, as other campers chose to use their free time to become voyeurs to our grudge match. More and more people crowded the court, sitting on sharp blades of dried grass and dirt. Their cheering and jeering were so loud I could barely hear Max agreeing to drop the weights when instructed. Even Greg's banter with his teammates slowed to a stop as he heard the sounds of the crowd gathering. He didn't look happy but marched over to our bench.

"You know, Max, I can add new rules, too." Greg jabbed.

Aaron, Richard, Darius, and Ira, like iron walls on a fortress, an imposing barricade of force stood at the sideline. This isn't a game of force, so I can't give them the Pitbull special. Today's game would be full of mind games and actual technical skills. Even a "Hail Mary" wasn't going to help us win. *Or perhaps it would.*

Max said to Greg grudgingly, "Your new rules? Well, spit 'em out, we ain't got all day." Max hissed. He did his best to steel his nerves, but flickers of worry still seeped at the corners of his eyes.

"If you're so quick to rush towards your demise, far be it from me to stop you." Greg blustered, circling the half-court we'd be playing on.

With his arms outcast to the growing audience, Greg began an oration.

"Today we will play a common basketball game called Horse. It's a simple game of Simon says. One captain takes a shot, and all the other players must take the same shot or acquire the first letter in the word HORSE. The shooter can take their shot anywhere in the half-court area. Simple, right?" Greg took a wide step to the three-point arc, used the ball tucked under his arm, and attempted a demonstration shot. *He missed.* A small wave of laughter rumbled through the audience.

He cleared his throat a few times and continued. "Play continues rotating to a new Simon from team to team until everyone on both teams has had a turn. Unlike our previous game, there won't be any opportunities to ride on coattails. Right, Pit?"

His smarmy tone made my blood boil, but when Greg looked at Max with a villainous smile, I wanted to punch him, and I'm not a violent man. *This show-boater was going down.*

Greg cackled. "Anyone who can't make that shot gets a letter, and these letters add up! New shot positions are earned only by completing the previous shot. Every missed shot gets a letter, and those who accumulate all the letters to spell HORSE will be eliminated. The person who has not spelled HORSE will be the winner."

This was all rudimentary stuff, but I had a Real Time Bill Mayer New Rules to add to this last-minute switch as well.

I stepped forward, asserting my height and weight on Greg's face. "I have a few new rules of my own, Greg. First, we don't have time for individual play. We'll play HORSE as a team. It's a one-on-one play from five positions, the final being the top of the key."

Greg bobbed his head, considering the new play. "Fine. What else?"

"Our next rule is that Max will be our final shooter against you at the top of the key. Your team can pick who they want to challenge first, and then it will be ours until all competitors have been chosen. This is non-negotiable." I stared him down, not flinching, though Max's eyebrows shot up in shock.

Greg raised his eyebrows, indicating he liked the twist in play, and confirmed it with a resounding, "You're on!" He raised his hand in the air, waiting for my high-five to prove we were ready to go, and I gave it gladly.

The game began without issue, though Malcolm and Dudley died a quick death alongside Aaron from Greg's side. Dudley's statistical prowess was useless in this challenge. Malcolm, let's just say, it wasn't his best day.

The next round of victims landed on Richard and Ira. They blew simple shots even my little sister could make. I was embarrassed for them. As much as basketball fundamentals are a vital part of the game, you need improvisational skills, and those two didn't, wildly missing the mark.

Next, it was my turn. I choked completely, whiffing the shot. I was knocked out of the game and banished to the sidelines, acting more like a color commentator to Max and Greg had to pull off a victory for their teams.

With all my guys benched when Walter missed his shot, it was up to Max to win the game. He stood on the sidelines the whole time, fidgeting his hands and pacing, barely looking at his teammates. He needed to get out of his head and remember that he could achieve anything he wanted. I couldn't be prouder of Max, especially since he still wore those weights. The impressive sportsmanship from our side was enough to make this grown man cry. Luckily, I'm not that grown man, so the tears stayed right where they were.

"Max!" I called out to him to get his attention and motioned for a time-out.

Max ran over, and I caught him behind his neck. "Both teams have H-O-R-S, so the next person that makes the shot, and one misses, that team gets the E to knock their team out. I stood over Max on the sideline and explained that changing from man to man to having teams was working out better than I thought.

Max looked up at me, horrified! I slapped his back to get his attention and get him focused. His soft smile crept from his mouth to his eyes, confirming he was on board with our plan. My boy was ready, and I sure as hell hoped I wasn't wrong.

He blinked, thought for a moment, and then ripped the weights off his wrists, letting them fall with a thump to the ground. His eyes widened, and he realized how light he felt swinging his arms and circling his wrists.

On the other hand, Greg fumed, realizing the handicap of those weights was the only thing holding Max back.

"What's that, Greg? Did you think this was going to be easy? Nice try." Max taunted him. "You are what we call cliché. Basic. A Neanderthal. I want to say you're unenlightened but showing you will be so much more fun." Max walked back to the designated spot and prepared to make his shot.

I'd expected Max to throw daggers with his eyes at Greg, but instead, he softened his stare and took pity on this fool. Greg would need more than a win to take advantage of Max again. My boychic was evolving, and I couldn't help but think my lessons were taking root. This is what the wish was all about.

17

THE DUEL

MAX

My arms felt light as a feather. *Hoo-baby!* Larry came through again. When Greg opened his mouth, all that looseness evaporated, and tension began to set in again.

"All right, Squirt, it's a jump shot from right here, top of the key. A small fry like you doesn't have a ghost of a chance making that." It would take more than Greg's condescending tone to get me down.

I grinned back, hoping to get under his skin. "We'll see, Homer." I cracked myself up at my Simpson's reference. Greg really did act like Homer.

His scowl read, 'I hit the mark'. *Good.*

I squared up to make the shot, something Larry and I had been practicing since camp began. I jumped up and pressed the ball into the air, letting it leave my fingertips evenly. In the past, I knew I didn't have a chance in hell at making this shot, but maybe...

Wait! Why the hell is it still in the air? Oh my God. It went over the backboard and bounced into a field. Greg's eyes widened, and a hush swept over the crowd, leaving me stunned and confused. *Did I do that?* I didn't get much chance to think about it when Greg squared up for the same shot. He jumped into the air, the ball flying in a near-perfect arc, but unfortunately for him, it hit the rim and dropped behind the foul line. *Not so perfect now, Mr. Big Shot.* Greg landed with a growl of disappointment, knowing I got to pick the next shot.

"All right, highflier, what's next?" he barked towards me. I considered my options and walked to the half-court circle, smashing the ball exactly where I wanted the shot to be taken. The crowd roared with anticipation. The new lightness in my arms allowed me to shoot so much farther than previously, and it was time to take advantage of it. I knew Greg was a strong player, though every time he got into his head, he made a mistake, and I was banking on it.

The look on Greg's face was priceless. Drained of color, his lips were pressed tightly together. However, his words were contradictory. "Easy money." He spat out. *It's not over 'til it's over, Greg.*

I prepared for the shot. I squared my body and held my breath, pushing through my legs and torso, up through my arms to the very tips of my fingers, and waited. The rush of wind pressing the net could be heard throughout the court, and the long-awaited swish pounded in my ears. A loud cheer from the crowd signaled my direct hit. I did it. I. Did. It!

I spun around in a circle, my hands on my head in disbelief, and my whole team stormed the court as if I'd won the game. Except, I hadn't— yet. I was one shot away from a draw if Greg made the shot or a clear winner if he missed.

Greg pressed his lips together and gave a small smile. Was he impressed?

I knew my dad would have gotten into Greg's head, taunting him with, "That basket is awfully far," or "Be careful of those gusts of wind; they'd mess with your shot." I could only imagine what was going through his head. Nerves? Annoyance? Fear?

Greg made his way into position, dribbling the ball three times. I couldn't help but shoot him a wisecrack as he lined up his shot.

"No pressure, Greg. It's a tough shot. Only one out of a hundred can make that shot. There's no shame in missing this. I'll still respect you." Greg bristled like a horse after a race.

Time stopped as the ball left his hands; the anticipated *whoosh* of the net couldn't come fast enough. And then—it fell in. We tied? I suppose we did. Then why did it feel like a win to me?

A rush of adrenaline blew through me. "YESSS!!" I shouted at the top of my lungs. I jumped up and down, whooping it up, feeling alive. Anguish washed over his face, and I took great joy as I smiled at him.

"Dude, that was amazing!" Dudley said, smacking me between my shoulder blades.

"That half-court shot was insane," Walter yelled animatedly. Malcolm shoved his hand in my direction like a business deal had been made.

"You did good. Nice work out there." He jutted his chin toward me, pursing his lips. It had an unusual look and a nice change from his straight-faced loner schtick.

Larry grabbed me on the shoulder and smiled brightly.

"I told you those weights would do the trick," he said confidently. Boy, did I have words for him.

"It did, but it also felt like high-grade sabotage. I had to refigure my strength as I did the shots." I said, exasperated. He looked offended, then smiled and jabbed my side.

Greg sauntered over, making my team take two steps back.

"I want to talk to you alone, Max." He said in hushed tones. My friends were leery about leaving me alone with him, mainly if he chose to beat the ever-loving shit out of me. Fortunately for me, his energy level morphed into a tone of respect. The cockiness was gone, and his voice didn't hiss anymore.

I looked at each of my friends, encouraging them to take off. "It's fine, guys, I'll catch up." Larry still looked reluctant to leave, eye-balling Greg like the Pitbull he was. Moments later, he backed down and stood ten feet away, just in case.

"What's up?" I offered.

"Looks like the Pitbull's influence has greatly improved your game. Maybe he has nothing to do with it. Either way, your attitude and leadership have given you an edge, and that works for you. Not to brag, but I've ruled this place for a while. It's not often someone rises to the challenge to take me on, but you did. When you get to this level of play, great plays and technique deserve respect. You know, game recognizes game."

Holy shit. Greg accepted me as a peer. I couldn't have seen this coming from a mile away. I barely let the following words stumble out of my mouth as I tried to figure out how to navigate this situation.

"Why are you telling me this?"

"Because, from now on, I'm cool with you winning. I need someone or a team that pushes me. Playing sports is more fun that way." He smacked his hand on his head. "God, this is why I don't like this sentimental shit." With his hands jammed to his hips, he pivoted away from me.

Could it be he's going through his own mental journey? After all, the empire he'd spent years building at school and camp was finally beginning to show cracks. I knew the best way to help him save face.

"So, a rivalry then? Yes, game recognizes the game. You're an insane athlete, Greg. You forced my friends and me to give everything to our gameplay so we could even have a chance to keep up with you and your friends. I respect that, and honestly, it lit a fire under my ass." I wanted to be as straightforward and honest to Greg in this conversation. He deserved it.

"I expect you to be the one who leads your team to victory. You can be co-captains with Pit all you like, but you're the one I'm watching my back for. Good luck, Max. For the record, this was fun at the end."

I had become an equal to Greg and felt like a superhero.

He walked past me toward his cabin, leaving me alone on the court for a few minutes. His words sunk in like sand into water. My only companions were the crickets and wind in the trees.

Sid waved to me to follow the others since hanging out alone wasn't allowed. The rustle of grass and leaves under my feet as I made my way back up the hill would be as close to calm as I'd feel this afternoon. Nature energized me, and I stopped at the top of the hill and looked out over the sports field. I breathed in and out, reveling in today's results, thinking of my dad again. His meditation had become my meditation. The day would come when I would have to admit to him how helpful this tool had become for me—just not now.

"I DID IT!" I shouted into the afternoon air, my back bending backward for only the open blue sky above to see and hear.

18

ESPIONAGE

LARRY

I t was a nice night to relax after today's challenge and celebratory festivities that rocketed Max to the top of the camper pool. We nerds earned more respect than ever, and nothing would dampen that achievement. Sports without rivalry isn't really a sport; it's just a game. I wished I could talk to Max about today's match as his father, but I couldn't blow my cover and disgrace him that way. I contemplated in bed what transpired over the past several days and the incredible improvement in my relationship with my son. My wish came true one hundred percent. The trick now was transferring that to reality.

Max seemed to thrive now that he'd found his confidence. He pushed past his fears of Greg, or at least came to terms with them. He excelled in two sports, utilizing new skills and good training.

Then why am I still worried? Why did I still feel like something was off? I'd forgotten to do something. What was it? *Shit! Shit! Shit! The letter.* In all my planning, I forgot the two-week check-up letter I always wrote to Max. How was I going to fix this? *Oy! More deep breathing.*

I reached under my bed for my duffle bag and rummaged around for some stationery. Maybe my dad thought to include it in the stuff he prepared. *Please, Dad! Did you pack it? Anything? Any scrap of paper will do. Is this it? Crap.* It's just my card that brought me back to my Howard form. Okay. I'd have to raid the craft building tomorrow and hope to find something that would work. For now, though, the panic mode would be turned off, and sleep mode would be turned on. I crossed my fingers, praying this glitch could be resolved quickly, and fell into a deep sleep.

Morning couldn't have come fast enough. My mind was already racing. Where was my phone? *Damn! I gave it to Dale!* Besides, we were probably too deep in the woods to get a decent connection. Okay. New plan. I'd go to the craft studio and find stuff to write a letter. As I put on my shoes, I realized my letter wouldn't have any canceled postage. This day got worse and worse.

I paced the floor several times and devised another new plan. I'd jog out of camp and find a gas station to make a call. Easy peasy.

I ran past the cabins, then up towards the mess hall and offices, where I ran into Sid.

"Hey, Larry. Where are you going so fast?" This guy saw everything.

I gulped. "Uh, uh, the infirmary. I think I have poison ivy." I punted for an excuse. This malady was plausible; hopefully, I could get my hands on a phone while I faked my problem.

"Sure thing. Don't touch anyone, though. It's contagious." He preached.

I looked astonished as if I was a clueless kid. "Oh my gosh. Okay. No touching anyone. Got it."

I turned tail and ran into the offices just over the hill.

The nurse was busy with another camper in the next room, and the camp phone was only a few feet away. I looked around the room, pulled the landline into the corner, and dialed Dale. I hoped to God he would pick up.

The line clicked on. Yes! "Hey Dale, this is Howie."

"Howie? Don't tell me they kicked you out of camp already?" I chuckled, imagining Dale's smarmy face.

"Listen. I don't have time to chat. I totally forgot to send Max his mid-camp letter. I'm taking a big chance using the camp's phone to contact you, so here's what I need you to do."

"Way to go, numb nuts."

"Don't push me, Dale. I haven't had a moment's peace since I got here. Please type out a letter and send it today to Camp Windy City. It should only take you five minutes, and in a day or two, he'll get it. Tell Max I said I love him and am sorry about the delay. Make up a bullshit excuse and remind him I'm looking forward to seeing him on Parent's Day. Nothing too *schmaltzy*, All right?"

"Got it. One Cover-Your-Ass letter coming up. Anything else?

I looked around again, noticing the kid leaving the exam room. "One more thing. I need you to call Ilene during work hours. Her calls usually go to voicemail, and she won't answer. When it goes to voicemail, play the message I left that goes, 'Having a great time golfing, I know you must be slammed at work. In case you're wondering, I sent Max a letter and am confirming with my brother that he will drop me off at camp to meet you both on Parents Day. Love Ya!'"

"Right, that one. You set up a hell of a system here, bro."

"Thanks. It's nice to know I can still pull off some of Dad's old tricks. Oh boy, gotta go."

"Hang in there, pal. You're doing great." The line went dead, and I carefully walked back and set the phone exactly how I found it.

The deed was done, and I finally could take today's first big breath. What the hell was I thinking that I could waltz out of camp? I was a freaking teenager, not an adult with free reign to do what I wanted. A revelation swept in as I reviewed each step of the past thirty minutes. This must be what Max felt like when I cut him off at the knees. Saying no to him when he wanted to have time alone or go someplace new was stifling him. Adults had freedom. Kids didn't. I found another reason to believe in Max—trusting him when I wasn't around.

   schmaltz – chicken fat

   schmaltzy – to fatten up

19

HEIGHTS

LARRY

With the letter incident behind me and Max living large at camp, I've finally been able to sleep, get up for an early morning walk, and chill with my son and his friends—my friends. *If they only knew.* Some would say the sound of crickets and birds chirping made them feel alive. For me, it was a cacophony of snorting, farting, and whining about the heat. *Kids.*

"Hey, hey, get up," Max hollered, already standing by the side of my bunk. He had a silly grin on his face. *Uh oh, I know that face.* That was the face even adults feared— excitement laced with thrill-seeking glee, and everyone had to participate.

"It's ropes course day!" He said in an excited whisper. "Better stretch out, Larry. You're going to need it."

Oh, God, no. Today was going to be a long one. First, a week of football boot camp, then another busting my butt on the basketball court, and now, I'll be swinging from trees. My only reprieve was that I was in a kid's body.

After breakfast, Max took me on a walk to the ropes course in the trees by the sports fields. Planks, ropes, rope ladders, and every kind of tactical clip hung from each apparatus. The lower courses were more my speed, but as I looked higher and higher, the danger loomed greater and greater. I may have mentioned I'd do anything for my son, but I did have my limits.

"Larry, I know you've hesitated about going on the ropes course for a while, but I want you to try it. The whole cabin will be there today, and I want to help you like you helped me— All of us, even Greg's cabin. We've got to show up in force." Max said, with his new-found confidence. As you said, Greg's got nothing on us, and today is no different. What is it with you that you won't even try?" His annoyance with me seeped through each word. I growled at Max, which made him step back.

"I just don't want to do it, so stop pushing! That's the end of the conversation!"

Max's eyes blew wide open, and his mouth trembled. "You sounded just like my dad when he gets angry." He rubbed his jaw, trying to understand my reluctance and angry tone. This wasn't how I wanted today to go. Hadn't I pushed him since I arrived? My fear of heights was no different than Max not wanting to lose to Greg. What was I afraid of?

I breathed in and spoke louder, which would probably come back to bite me when I'd lost my voice. "I am one hundred and fifty pounds, and you're only seventy-five! That's a lot of weight falling from a rope hitting the ground. Getting pushed around on solid earth is much easier than breaking an arm or leg falling from a tree." *That was a genuine concern, though not the biggest one.*

Max responded with an understanding voice, "So you're scared? Do you mean you lack the confidence to even try? Do you mean you want to quit and not challenge yourself?" I could tell he was trying to keep his cool with me until he raised his voice and jammed his hands on his hips. "You stand here yelling at me because it's hard? Everything you've ever taught me was to build my confidence, insisting it started with changing my attitude, 'Never say can't or won't' or 'Don't give up before you put your best foot forward.' Was that all bullshit? Are you so afraid you can't follow your coaching advice?"

Max sounded more like his mother at this moment. Ilene could dismantle a person's argument in seconds to find the truth, making me more vulnerable and exposed. This was a moment for the books. The student had become the master, and the master the pupil. *How ironic.*

"Stand up, Larry," Max demanded, not taking no for an answer. It was his turn to take control, not yelling but speaking confidently.

"Don't make me remind you again how you turned my sorry ass into a confident fighting machine. I may only be seventy-five pounds, Larry, but you've opened my eyes to my potential, and I'll never forget that. Today's challenge, my friend, is a two-person rope course, and I will not be taking no for an answer. Teammates to the end!

Max looked confident enough for both of us. This was the moment that would define our future. Could I trust my life to him? Would he listen to my concerns and hear what I was saying? This was the biggest lesson I had learned so far. Maybe I wasn't the only one with correct answers. I promised to be a better listener, and I could hear my father laughing in Heaven at how the tables had turned. *Hilarious, dad.*

He grabbed my arm and pulled me to the harnessing area, where the ropes specialists walked us through the challenge.

"Hey, guys. I'm Rick, and this is Dan. Now that you're ready, let me remind you that ropes are about safety first and trust second. Check and double-check each carabiner closely before you step off. When transitioning, you must have two carabiners clipped onto your harness to ensure you are locked onto the next section. No exceptions. We will be watching." Rick demonstrated how to make a "legal" transition from one section to another using Dan as his dummy.

Rick pointed at me and Larry. "You two will be tied together with a six-foot piece of rope. You'll move through the obstacle course together, communicating every step of the way. Each team will be timed, and the fastest team will win a prize. Remember, safety first. Those not following the safety rules will be disqualified. Any team found cheating will be subject to disciplinary action. No pushing, shoving, or skipping sections. Got it? Let's go!"

I listened to Rick's speech, my head spinning about the rules and fighting the nausea from being forced to do something beyond my comfort zone.

"What?!" I scream out. "No practice runs? No strategizing?" I could feel the sweat building up all over my body. I could barely see as rivulets of sweat blinded me.

Max patted my back, laughing devilishly. His eyes narrowed at something even though he kept talking.

"You'll get to practice, but strategizing? Nah, this is simple. It's pretty basic: just put one foot in front of the other and try not to fall. You're athletic, Larry, so fess up. What's really the problem?"

How does the saying go, "The truth will set you free?" *Or kill you.*

I pulled Max close and whispered in his ear.

"I'm only telling you this because I trust you, but if you tell anyone else, I'll sit on your head and fart on you." We laughed until our eyes watered. That little bit of tension release was all I needed to give it to him straight.

"The real reason I can't do this is that I am afraid of heights."

Max's face changed in dawning realization. I didn't even know how I became afraid of heights, except my brothers would taunt me that they would sign me up for skydiving as a birthday gift. Their chiding always sets me off for some reason. The image of myself flying through the air and the ground so far away made me nauseous. That sinking feeling of air rushing past me as I plummeted to the earth made me sick to my stomach. The idea of my blood and guts splattering across the ground was pure panic. And, from that day on, I was afraid of heights.

Max revealed his feelings about the situation in a soothing, quiet tone.

"I was afraid of everything when I was little, but when my dad opened his big arms, I could get one of his big bear hugs, and all those fears melted away. He would always say he would protect me from all the bullies and chase all the monsters away when I was in that hug. I'm going to do the same for you. Would you like one of those hugs, Larry?" My eyes began to swell with tears. This was so important to me. Maybe that's what I misunderstood. He wanted comfort when he felt down. He wanted safety when he was unsure. It was something warm to come home to after being out in the cold and learning about the harsh world for himself. I let Max give me a great big bear hug even if his arms didn't exactly fit around me.

Mmm. "I'll take your hug and raise you two back. I truly appreciate the gesture, Max. I don't care what people say about you. You're one cool dude. Even if you have short arms." He punched me in the arm right before he launched himself into my chest.

"But I am still afraid of heights." I pleaded. Max released himself from the hug and rolled his eyes.

"Do I have to go to the Warriors Cabin and tell Greg that big bad Larry is too chicken to climb the ropes? Or are you going to suck it up, follow me, and listen to what I tell you? We'll do the best we can, right?"

"We won't win!"

"So, what!" Max yelled back, "We might fail, but we fail together as a team. That's all I care about."

"Fine," I responded weakly. My frown twisted into a smile and crept to my eyes as I walked away.

"When did you become so tough?" I chided. Max cackled into the morning air, apparently amused.

"You created a monster."

It was time for lunch, so with the practice and internal revelations rumbling within, we returned to the main camp and discussed how we would tackle the ropes course.

Greg apparently saw us settling in to eat lunch and decided now was a good time to razz us some more.

"Good morning, gentlemen. I'm excited about the ropes course today between our cabins. It's going to be hilarious." *Same shit, different day.*

Max took the bait. "What makes it so hysterical?"

"Oh, nothing. Only it's that I love the idea of the two of you tied together with such a weight difference between you, you know? Moving across and up and down will be great entertainment. Watching the two of you fail will be the highlight of my day. The camp coordinator loved my idea with the new caveat of a two-person team tied together. This will make an even greater challenge than last year." Greg said with pure spite streaked across his face.

Huh? Greg was the reason that we would be tied together. I shouldn't be surprised he'd find another reason to make a fun activity miserable. His assessment of our weight differential was accurate, though. I would hold Max back on this challenge, but there was no way to back out without crushing Max's feelings.

"Or am I wrong that you two will be competing together? After all, the two of you have been joined at the hip this whole time at camp. We've all assumed you may even shower and sleep together." Greg laughed, cracking himself up. "See you losers later today. And don't even think about wimping out!"

"Wouldn't dream of it!" Max yelled back.

I pulled Max aside, confused about his reaction to Greg's challenge. "What the hell was that?"

"I'm not at liberty to give you details, but know that Greg and I have come to an understanding. We won't be friends but respectful rivals. That's all."

"Seriously?"

"Let's call it a win-win for now. At least he won't try to kill me on the ropes course."

My poor decision to eat twelve pancakes, raw scrambled eggs, and partially cooked bacon, coupled with the realization I would soon be forty feet in the air, catapulted me out of my seat, racing to the latrines before I soiled myself. I barely made it to my porcelain throne before I embarrassed myself. My internal dialogue was harsh, but it was exactly what I needed.

Come on, Howard. Stop being a wuss. You can do this. You've done everything else this camp has thrown at you, including the questionable food. There's nothing to worry about. Think happy thoughts. Let the evil thoughts drop into the toilet. Oh, that's much better. There's nothing better than a morning constitutional. Now, bring on the day!

Max trotted down the hill to the ropes course like a champion thoroughbred. I've tried to psyche myself up, though fear still lurked about. As a forty-five-year-old man, I had a gait similar to an aged donkey ready for the slaughter. But here, in the barely worn suit of a thirteen-year-old, the only thing I feel is my waning courage. I'm taking bets on myself that this challenge will go better than I think it will.

The campers continue to sit in the "Us" vs. "Them" sections this summer. It's so sad that they feel that taking sides would make them feel more accepted. Camp was supposed to be fun, without care. But I was severely wrong in my estimation. Why Max continued to beg to come here was a puzzle I'd like to solve.

Like most camp days in late June, it was bright, sunny, and hot. The morning dew had long since evaporated, and the humidity was getting more oppressive every minute. The good news was that most of the course was under or in the trees, casting long shadows on the non-participating campers below.

Rick pulled a megaphone to his face and began calling for attention.

"Settle down, Campers!" as the kids smacked each other to stop talking. "Like everything this year, we have some new rules, so listen up. There can only be one team on the course at a time. Each team will be timed and then posted. All times will be revealed at the end, so no one has an advantage. The fastest time on the course will win. Failure to complete the course, fall off the course, or skip any part of the challenge will be an automatic disqualification. Is that clear? Every team shouted in the affirmative.

I looked at Max with trepidation, my peacefulness obliterated "What do they mean by that?"

"Disregard that middle part. We're going to be tethered to a rope with high-grade climbing gear. Even if we fall, we'll be safe and suspended up there. Either the counselors will help us back onto the course or help us get down from there easily," Max explained calmly.

"I feel so much better knowing we won't plummet to our death," I said, rolling my eyes.

"Larry, I'm using the new analytical skill you taught me to calculate where we'll need to work more closely. Since Greg snuck in a new rule, I countered with my own tactic: we get to go last. They may not tell us the exact finish times of each team, but my watch will. We'll only have to shave off a couple of seconds just to be sure. We can win this, Larry. Just believe."

"Win?" I laughed like a hyena. "I plan to be up there all night. But I will follow you and do the best I can because that's really all I can do at this point."

Max patted my back. "That's all I'm asking for."

Max and I watched every team work through the course. Most moved slowly and awkwardly through the challenge, up and down and back and forth, yet I still had no idea how we would handle this challenge. Greg's team was announced after most of the teams went through the course, and with practiced movements and insane athleticism, he and his partner, Ira, flew through the course as if they were trapeze artists from the circus. It was both beautiful and terrifying.

It was evident that, by the record time shown on my watch, Greg and Ira had set the bar for us to overtake. Their well-deserved bow as they ziplined down from the course and landed at the finish with nary a sweat on them was impressive. Rick announced that the last contestants were Max and me.

I could feel my own heart pumping and by the look on Max's red face, he was feeling the adrenaline, too. It didn't help that every camper at camp was either rooting or laughing at us. This made me a little nervous, even as our cabins cheered and jeered at us. Max turned to the crowd with his fisted arms up above his head as if he were Rocky Balboa, releasing a battle cry, "Here we go!" I fought the urge to run away, wanting to make my son proud of me. Maybe this might not be so bad.

Dan came around to inspect our equipment and tie off the six-foot rope between us. "Remember you guys, safety first. Communicate, and don't be a hero. It's summer camp, not the Olympics." He winked at us as Max bounced like he was entering a boxing ring. *Now that's a sport we should try.*

"Just follow my footwork, Larry, and we'll finish in no time. 'Keep punching.'" Max nodded to me, extending his right fist for a fist bump, the other guarding his face.

"If you say so," sighing heavily. It was time again for my breathing exercise. I needed to center myself like I never had before, even for my father's wish. I couldn't start this challenge with pessimism. I had to conquer my fear of heights—conquer my fear of humiliation when I became a laughingstock, falling from the course and letting my son down. It was go-time. Fears be damned!

Max grabbed the back of my harness and spun me around. "Here's the plan, Larry. The first two legs are super easy. Let's fly through those quickly, and then we'll have more time for the more intricate part of the course. Cool?"

"If you say so," I said nervously.

"Remember our Jamaican bobsled mantra? Feel the rhythm. Feel the rhyme?"

I nodded, and Max continued. "That's exactly how we'll attack the rest of the course. Stay loose. Become one with the ropes. We've got this."

Max made a compelling speech, but he didn't understand physics or the implications of an unbalanced system. I guess it's time for Einstein's Theory of Relativity to rear its ugly head.

We cleared the first two legs like Max spelled out. We were doing great until a voice pierced through my brain.

"Hey, dinner is served in a few hours. As much fun as it is to watch you two clowns up there, I'd rather eat."

I was drawn to Greg's shit-eating grin from below and wobbled on the landing pad. *Jerk!*

Greg's team finished with a shocking nine-minute camp record. Unless I became a monkey, there was a ten to twenty percent chance we'd beat their time.

I was straining, sweating, and swearing every obscene word and gesture I could muster, realizing I wasn't made for this activity. Max kept encouraging me occasionally but couldn't control his annoyance at our slow progress. We looked like a sideshow at a circus the way I flailed my arms and legs every other minute.

We finally got up to the top layer and started to make our way across the final obstacles. You know that feeling that something terrible was about to happen nanoseconds before it did? Well, it did. Shooting pains tore through my right calf. It was the worst Charley horse I'd ever had. It was destroying me.

"LEG CRAMP!!"

As I reached down to massage my leg, the next domino fell in my chain of regrets. Max's eyes widened because as I fell, the rope between us dragged Max off the course, leaving us looking like a pair of tennis shoes with laces tied together swinging from the main rope hanging above us. Did I mention the physics differential? Max hung just under the main line while I hung three feet below him. Max's uncontrollable laughter aggravated me.

I'm glad he was having a great time, but I screamed in terror, fighting the searing pain of my leg and the utter humiliation I knew would happen, wondering how the hell we'd get out of this situation.

It took a few minutes, but my heart rate settled, and I looked around. There was no real fear of falling, and my terror turned to tears of laughter. Our predicament was comedy gold, as exhibited by the peals of laughter from below. It humbled me. Big guys like me needed to stick to earth-bound endeavors and leave the lithe ones to swing through the trees. This was another glorious memory from camp I'd never forget.

"Larry, your weight is pulling my side so tight. Untie the rope. Otherwise, I am going to suffocate, and we are not going to be able to get back up to at least finish. It looks like help is on the way and once we get you back up we'll finish solo, not tied together." Max wheezed his instructions.

"Sorry, buddy. Give me a second." I grinned and released the rope around my waist, and in a matter of seconds, Max got his feet back on the course and, with some grit and muscle Sid sent up, they pulled me up easily. With careful pivoting and leveraging, we pulled ourselves over to the rappelling landing, where we caught our breath.

"Are you ready for the best ride of your life, Larry?" Max bit his lip and nodded his head. He knew what was coming next, and I hadn't a clue.

"Is it better than hanging like dirty laundry on a line?" I cackled.

"So much better!" A second later, he had transferred his carabiner off the main line to the rappelling line, yelling as he went. "Cowabunga!!"

I repeated the steps and yelled something entirely different, "Holy shit!"

Greg ran over to the end of the course as we unclipped from the ropes and harnesses and handed them off to Dan.

"That's the best thing that has happened at camp this whole season. You two are hilarious," Greg said, grinning ear to ear. We shook hands, and when he left, Max and I hugged it out once again. I couldn't wait to sit down. The adrenaline was wearing off, and I was feeling woozy. We sat on a bench together, recounting every moment through the ropes course; the highs and the lows. Sharing time with Max was what every father would want with his son.

I stared into space, reflecting. "I hate how you pushed me into something I didn't want to do. I knew I wouldn't be good at it. I'm not made for that kind of stuff. But, once you told me how your dad would do the same things to you, I now understand why you view your dad as being so selfish, stubborn, and hurtful. I get why you don't like your dad."

"Wait a second!" Max yelled. "I never told you I don't like my dad! My dad is and always will be my best friend. It's just that sometimes we disagree on how we look at life. When it comes to pushing me into things I don't think I could be good at, my dad is my best cheerleader, along with my mom. He would get me more if he could see the world more through my eyes and not his life's journey. Does that make sense?" He picked at the dried grass, folding it between his fingers just like I did.

I began to tear up. I didn't know how to respond. My heart broke knowing how he truly felt about me. Giant blobs of water gushed downward at all the horrible mistakes I made raising my son. I thought my father's way was the right way to raise a son. The *only* way to raise a son. I've gone about all of this completely wrong.

"Are you crying, Larry?" Max asked, looking over at me.

"No, I must have gotten something in my eye when I sat on the ground."

"Sure, Spock, whatever you say." The Star Trek reference got me smiling again amidst the tears. I stood up and grabbed Max, yanking him into a classic big bear hug.

"You can hug me anytime to protect me from all the bullies and chase all the monsters in the world away, Kirk." Max blinked, looking at me funny.

"Stop hugging me before Greg sees us." He started to push me away when I retaliated with my push, sending him to the ground. I still didn't know my strength after all this nonsense at camp.

As I helped him, I quietly chuckled, "You're such a Boychic!"

"What?" Max looked confused as he took my hand.

"Luke, I am your father." My hand slid to my face to muffle my voice like Darth Vader.

"Noooo!!" He yelled back and ran up the hill towards the main camp.

20

TIME PASSES

LARRY

G reg and Ira won the ropes prize. I didn't envy them. I was glad we didn't win. The prize was a day at the lake with the counselors-in-training. If there was anything that scared me more than heights, it was being dragged behind a speedboat. *Dear God! Who the hell thought that was a good idea?* Visions of me skidding across the water and sinking like a stone gave me night sweats. The embarrassment of explaining this to Max was more than I could take. Thankfully, he wasn't too keen on the idea either.

The following week passed without a hitch. Days filled with camp games and small events, culminating in a day trip to a nearby city to see a movie, were outstanding. *Can you say air conditioning?*

The bus ride into town allowed us to smack talk and goof around, cementing our relationships. Stephen showed us something so revolting that I almost gagged. Apparently, he could shoot a snot rocket up to three feet!

On another day, Dudley saved the day by coming up with an impossible answer only his savant brain could retrieve during a game of trivia. Then, two days ago, we bet Malcolm he couldn't sing on Karaoke night, but he wowed us as he sang the oldie "Welcome to The Jungle" by Guns N' Roses. He proved us wrong, and our punishment for not believing in him was to scour the cabin before Parent's Day.

This whole camp experience was something I'd never taken for granted. If it weren't for the fact I was living in a kid's body, I wouldn't have made it. All those sporting contests weren't half as bad as navigating bullies, bad attitudes, and bad food. I loved it all! The idea of going back to my former self made me a little weepy. I'm not going to lie.

Greg's cabin started warming up to ours after all the recent challenges. Respect was earned and given, and I'm sure the boys felt a new appreciation for everyone's contribution to the team. These were precious bubbles in time we all savored as we grew up. Watching Max figure things out, making new friends, and growing as a human and friend were some hallmarks I'd cherish, and he would, too.

"Hey, Max!" I smiled, walking over to our cabin table.

"Morning, Larry. You're looking excited. What's up?" Max said, stuffing his face with cereal.

"I checked the forecast today. It's a good day to go on the trails."

"Like, for hiking? Yeah, that might be fun."

"How about mountain biking?" *I can't believe I never taught my kid how to ride a bike. It was a rite of passage; again, I felt like a failure to my son.*

"Nah, not for me." Max shook his head.

"C'mon, I know you told me no before because you like rollerblading more, but it's the perfect day for biking on the trails!" I pleaded.

"And like I said before, the answer is still no. Let it go."

I understand he's annoyed, but I put myself way out of my comfort zone yesterday for him. It's his turn to step it up.

Greg sauntered over, looking smug, "You're going mountain biking?"

"I asked Max if he wanted to go on the trails today but wasn't interested, so I will probably hike on them instead," I said, biting the inside of my cheek.

Greg wasn't giving up. "My cabin is going mountain biking after breakfast. You should join us." I thought about his offer but I still couldn't tell if he was being genuine or trying to lure me into a ravine and break my kneecaps.

"Thanks for the offer, but I'm going to pass. I'm going to hang with my cabin today. Maybe go for a swim.

"Fine. Your choice. Good luck next week. You're going down." Greg marched away, smug as usual.

I looked at Max's ashen face. "What did he mean by that?"

"Next week is camp competition week. Various sports are being played for the last few days of camp, culminating in a final event on Parent's Day."

"Oh. ...oh wow." I began pacing. We needed to start training fast. Greg had been training the whole session, and if we didn't figure out a full-proof plan, we were screwed. I looked at the rest of the cabin, assessing our weak skill set.

I stopped and looked straight at Greg's still smug face, "Thanks for the heads-up. I know you didn't have to say anything, but I really appreciate it. May the best team win." As a good-faith gesture, I shoved my hand before me, not expecting him to grab hold so tightly.

"You'd better give me a run for my money." My hand winced as he locked down on mine tightly. I nodded quickly, hoping the blood would return just as fast. He then turned his attention to Max.

"Remember our deal?" Greg used his two fingers, pointing from his eyes to Max's, and walked back to his friends, not waiting for a reply.

My friends assembled closely around me.

"Grab your racquets, fellas. It's time to prepare for another showdown." *We'd had more of those than a Western drama.*

21

GAME

LARRY

As a thirteen-year-old, I was exhausted both physically and mentally. My wisdom as a forty-five-year-old was the only thing keeping me focused on getting through this week and earning another win for my cabin. I'd dreamt of barbequing in my backyard for three nights and napping in my big, comfy chair. Good food and comfortable sleep spaces are no laughing matter when you're deprived of both for three weeks. Camp had been a blast, but I looked forward to being my old self again.

Earlier this morning, each cabin was instructed to select a team captain and co-captain for this week's final events.

"Here we go again, guys. Who wants to be captain and co-captain? Hurry up because Sid needs you both in his office for a meeting."

After ten seconds of head swivels from every guy, I stood forward, pulling Max to my side.

"I guess it's us again. Surprise!" I lightly punched Max in the shoulder, and he punched me back. *I really hoped we could continue being close like this next week when this whole façade was over.*

Sid sat mulling over some papers scattered over his desk, ignoring a herd of kids bombarding his office. Camp survival gear hung on the far wall, while the opposite wall had a visual timeline of camper photos from every session back to its inception. Along with Max and me, each set of captains with their assigned counselor formed a cluster and came to attention when Sid rose from his desk.

"I've taken some of your suggestions of which sport would be best for each age group, but who came up with wrestling? Seriously? And, while rock climbing is challenging and exciting, have any of you seen a climbing wall at this camp? The biggest hill we have is the one to the sports field. With all due respect, people, let's pick something I don't have to spend ten thousand dollars on and a rider for my insurance policy, Okay?"

While I understood what Sid described, these kids stood there like he spoke a foreign language. *Insurance riders?*

I stepped forward respectfully. "What if the younger cabins played a two-on-two tennis match while the teenagers played a one-on-one? All the finalists could play on Parent's Day." Sid rubbed his jaw with one hand and wrapped the other around his chest.

"I like it. It will give the parents something to support," Sid said, admitting with a nod. He wrote the event on his itinerary sheet: 'Tennis Match.' "I need more ideas, though. Not everyone's going to want to do tennis."

Sid quieted the group down again, asking for more last-day options. With little negotiation, the team leaders came up with one other alternative non-competitive event: a visual art show in the arts and crafts building and another competitive event: kayaking down at the waterfront. There was something for everyone. The day would culminate with a camper/parent capture-the-flag event that I've been told is a long-standing camp tradition.

"Gather around men. Most of you know what this week means. Since this is my first go-around, I will need everyone to step up and give me all your intel on each opponent's tennis strengths and weaknesses. I want to know what they're eating, their training, and what other campers are saying behind our backs. Got it?" I barked my order like a true Master Sergeant.

Any little piece of information could make our strategy stronger.

My battalion of not-so-good tennis players marched to the courts, awaiting our following directions. We didn't have to wait long when our counselor, Dave, approached us.

"For those who don't have your own racquet, go to the fieldhouse and find one. We'll start practicing when we know what the itinerary looks like. The rest of you, start stretching." Our cabin was tight. They knew what was coming and what was expected of them. Max and I had our work cut out for us again. The good news was we knew who the players were and how to rattle them with mental warfare.

There wasn't any pushback from either the campers or counselors. Tennis was my jam, and I knew I could whip our representative into place in a few days.

Max whispered, "You've got to be the anchor and play against Greg. You know more about this sport and more about Greg's game than I do. Please, Larry. Do this for me." Max's pleas were rather pathetic, and I was about to concede when I remembered I had to be Howard on Parent's Day. Not Larry. *That was a close call.*

"Not a chance, Buddy. This is your summer to shine. Think about it, Max. Everyone loves an underdog story. It'll be great seeing you show your parents how far you've come on your final day of camp.

Five minutes later, we reversed ourselves out of Sid's office, all hyped about our final competitions.

I spun Max around and pointed my finger directly at his face. "You're to face off with Greg by the end of the week. End of story."

Yeah. I didn't think he would let this go. "You're sounding like my dad again. It's unbelievable how similar you are to him. It's freaking me out." Max mumbled his last words, slumping on an oversized rock and staring at the trees. "Now what? Is it time for another one of your training schemes to make things miraculously work out?"

His sarcasm was warranted. I had a million lessons to teach him but so little time. It was time to pull out every stop and drive home the lessons I'd been beating into him and his friends all month.

"Pretty much. Besides, you've at least played the game before, so you're not coming in from scratch. Do you trust me enough to know that I wouldn't put you in a situation where you're destined to embarrass yourself? I believe in you, Max, and like before, I want you to believe in yourself, too." Max sighed in resignation.

I yanked his hand to help him back to standing.

"You're lucky that you're my best friend, Spock." He snorted and shook his head.

"I wouldn't have it any other way, Kirk." I knocked his shoulder with mine. "Come on. We've got to go save the galaxy."

22

SET

LARRY

We huddled around a tree halfway down to the sports fields while I explained how the competition would go. The guys understood that not everyone would be playing on Parent's Day. Some sighed their relief, while others looked annoyed. Most kids like showing off for their parents, but some only feel their scrutiny and would instead wash toilets rather than subject themselves to that.

"Sid is allowing us to choose who plays in which bracket for the opening competition starting in eight days. We won't know the other cabin's lineup, and they won't know ours. First, if anyone would rather do kayaking or visual arts, please tell me now; otherwise, you're playing tennis. I paced back and forth, waiting for any raised hands or for the door to thwack shut. *None of the above. Good.*

"Great! Let's get to work."

"Max, put your racquet away. You'll be using mine." I reached into my bag, unzipped the cover, turned, and thrust it into his chest.

"What? Why?" His forehead furrowed, and his face began to redden.

This was my last chance to teach my son what I knew without being his dad. One he should already know from years playing tennis—if he had listened to his coaches—or me.

"Your racquet may be more expensive, but with my racquet, you will learn to make the ball dance off the strings. I will teach you how to use dinks, drop shots, side spins, under spins, lobs, and be able to strike with tremendous power when needed." I pointed to the racquet now tucked under his armpit.

"That is the classic Jimmy Connors metal racquet, the famous T2000."

Max stared. "It looks like a badminton racquet. That thing is older than my dad." *He wasn't wrong.*

"This racquet is strung with lamb gut, board tight, and believe me when I tell you, you will shock the shit out of Greg if you follow my instructions and work hard."

We had eight days to practice, and the game was about accuracy.

"Hey, I need three of you to stand at positions one, two, and three right at the net equal distance apart." Larry pointed to three equidistant places in front of the net. "Walter, get to the fourth position in the middle of the court. Nicky and Ernie get on the baseline on opposite sides. Got it?"

"Got it." The group responded in unison.

Once the guys were in place, I called out the drill.

"Each one of you is a target. I'll call a number, and Max will aim the ball at you. Coordination will be the name of the game. You'll need to stay light, stay on your toes, and stay focused on the ball at all times. After five balls, we'll rotate so everyone gets a turn. Understand?"

The drill began, and fifteen minutes later, we finished one circuit.

"Let's step it up, guys. You'd better be running between turns, and I want you shifting on your feet the whole time. No. Standing. Still. Let's go!"

Max grimaced. "This racquet is surprisingly heavy, though I'm impressed at how much more power it gives me than mine. Honestly, I'm tired of questioning you and your methods, Larry. You're never wrong, and it's annoying even if it brings us another victory." *From your mouth to God's ears. Finally!*

After each man had three turns, it was time to shift gears—serving.

I stood next to a basket of balls and demonstrated a textbook serve. Dudley studied me as I threw another ball in the air while Ernie waved a hand in front of his mouth, yawning. *Was anyone taking this seriously?*

"Hello? Are you guys even paying attention? If you're too tired, get off the court. I know what I'm doing, but do you? You're playing one-on-one. There's no one to cover your ass on this challenge, and I don't have time to waste on you if you aren't working harder than the guy next to you."

That's all it took for four guys to leave the court. *Good. Now I know who wants to win their match.*

With our focus in the right place, I began the next drill. "All right, now we're going to have you return serves. I'll toss a ball at you all day, but you'd better be ready when you get in front of Greg and need to return a serve from that powerhouse." Max nodded in agreement. He was determined and ready. The guys lined up on the opposite side of the net near the baseline. Serve after serve, I strategically forced each player to anticipate their movement and stay on their toes.

"The serves are so hard!" Max cried. "I need to play way back here even to have a chance to return them."

"Wrong, wrong, wrong. Meet me near the net." I grabbed Max's wrist and dragged him behind me. "The T2000 will allow you to short-hop Greg's serve and drive him absolutely crazy." Max contemplated the strategy and set himself up at half court, awaiting his next serve.

I instructed. "Keep the racquet square in front of you. Quickly jab at those short shots, throwing off your opponent's pacing. They'll expect you to run for the ball when you're breaking its path driving down the line. Easy peasy."

Max shuffled his feet back to his starting position.

"Don't get frustrated, Max. You've got this. Try again," I encouraged him

"Fine."

Watching Max play dodgeball while I pummeled him with serves was painful, but after a dozen tries, he stepped forward and jabbed at the ball off the bounce to drive home a winning shot. *Finally! A short hop I could be proud of.*

"Everything is easy peasy with you, Larry. Some of us have to work harder than others." He snickered, giving me some lip. "Show me what else I can do with this T2000." *This is what I'd been waiting for—his eagerness to learn from me.*

Every day was the same. Up at six-thirty, practice until eight, shower and breakfast by nine, and then regular camp activities. Free time became training time, and evening activities were mandatory full-camp events. Sid was a stickler about not overdoing practice times. Camp was for fun, relaxation, and healthy competition. I'm sorry to inform him that this year's camper experience in our cabin was about turning boys into men—focused, skilled, fighting machines. *Yeah, I went a little overboard there.*

Max asked questions like I drilled my serves—hard and non-stop.

"How do I hit a drop shot? A lob dink, an underspin?" All his questions were right on point.

It was time for a water break and some planning. We sat on the sidelines in the shade while the other guys took turns lobbing the balls over the net while I volleyed strategy into Max's ear.

"I've watched Greg practice for a few weeks now. When someone hits a high lob, he uses his overhead smash. Every time Greg hits that shot, you'll notice he celebrates with a clenched fist pump."

Max sardonically responded, "So that's a hard no to a high lob?

"No, no," I waved a finger at him. "I want you to hit him as many high lobs as you can on non-game winning points. We want Greg to feel confident and comfortable every time he charges the net, so you set him up with a high lob for his overhead smash, but again, never on a game-winning point." I stared at Max, waiting for the proverbial light bulb to kick on. *There it is.*

"You're one crafty son of a bitch, Larry." He winked at me, and I finally took a deep breath. He was getting it.

"Once the match starts and it's your serve, pick your serve and drill it down the middle for an ace. Your power will shock the shit out of him. You are a force to be reckoned with! Then, there's the sidespin serve.

You'll strike the ball on its side as it drops, creating a spin that will deflect the ball out to the side fence when it hits the surface. He won't have a chance to return the ball, right? The way to beat Greg is to outsmart and outplay him. Get into his head and keep him guessing your next move. Keep Greg off his game and you'll control everything."

I could only imagine how all the intricacies of having a solid strategy could boggle the mind.

"Larry, I'm picking up what you're putting down, but I don't want you to get mad if I forget something. You're shoving a lot of knowledge down my throat, and I can only digest so much at one time. I promise to do my best and still have fun."

"Visualize your shots, practice your footwork, decide ahead of time how you plan to handle your receiving shots and anticipate anything and everything. Tennis is a finesse game. Don't overthink every shot. You've got this. Max, the T2000 is the equivalent of a concert violin. It knows what to do so long as the user does.

"Serve me a ball. I want to show you something I picked up." Max proclaimed, jumping from his seat and grabbing his racquet.

We walked over to the court and kicked the other guys off to rest. I walked to the court's far side, bounced the ball a couple of times, and prepared to serve. Max bounced from foot to foot, waiting to receive, then returned the ball with his double forehand, crushing it down the line.

I was shocked at how fast and accurate that shot was. We'd found his money shot.

"Unbelievable! Why have you been holding that shot back from me?"

"You never asked what my best shot was." He replied smugly.

"Max, that is a fantastic shot, but please note, "Never use that shot during the set." I implored him.

I stood back, giving the kid some space. I knew I was giving him a masterclass in tennis skills and strategy and expected him to absorb every bit of it and then deliver on it. My expectations were *way* over the top, and I knew it. I don't know why I pushed him so hard, but I could barely stop myself.

"What?" Max answered meekly.

I looked at Max, pleading, "Every shot has a time and place, and if you reveal your double-handed forehand too early, he'll know what you're up to. That has to be your big finale—Game. Set. Match."

"All right, I understand why you're saying that, but I'd appreciate you not riding me so hard." He walked off the court miffed, then looked over his shoulder, surprising me.

"Hey, Larry. I appreciate you. Thanks for pushing me to be my best. Let's have fun at Parent's Day, huh?"

I waved and shouted back, "Winning *is* fun, Max."

23

MATCH

MAX

Training was over, camp was almost over, and so was my time with my buddies and new best friend, Larry. So many unpredictable things happened to me at camp this summer. Things that amazed me. Things that scared me. Mostly I felt transformed. I felt different. I thought differently, and my outlook on life was boosted. I felt alive and seen.

Today's competition would be another one of those world-shifting moments, and I was ready.

The stands of the tennis courts were filled and I craned my neck to find my parents, but I could only see my mom. *Figures.* Sid walked out to the middle of the tennis court and announced and waited for everyone to quiet down.

"How have you all enjoyed the matches so far?" Sid paused while the crowd roared, "Your kids have been amazing this season, and as you can see, they have banded together to support each other in our final tennis match. For those who are interested in visual arts, please stop by the Arts and Crafts building to see a tremendous art exhibit this session's campers have created. I know I will."

Several parents nodded their heads, giving in to Sid's suggestion. "We've seen your younger campers tear up this surface, now it's time for our teenage headliners, Greg and Max. Both young men have been battling each other on the football field, basketball court, and now, the tennis court."

Sid marched up and down the sideline, telling our parents about sportsmanship and camaraderie and how we all needed to come back next year. Sure, I get all of that, but I just wanted to start our match before I puked.

I looked again at the crowd where I found my mom, but I still couldn't see my dad. I looked the other way and found Greg tapping his hand against his racquet strings. *I bet he didn't feel like puking.* It didn't bother me as much as it used to that Greg was so athletically awesome. After all the bullying he dished out and all the training Larry dished out, earning respect from both of them was the biggest prize of all. I knew that no matter what happened today, I knew I was awesome, too. My Dad always said that once you conquer the big guy, the weak will fall.

"Ladies and Gentlemen, this will be a one-set match! In the event the score goes to a 6-6 tie, there will be a one-game tiebreaker. Everything else is standard tennis stuff. May the force be with both of you!" Sid finished with his own Star Wars reference.

The crowd laughed, leaving me and Greg to find our places on the court. As I grabbed a small towel to wipe my forehead, I heard Larry creep up behind me.

"Max!" Larry whisper-yelled, probably for one last pep talk.

"You've got this. You have all the skills to whoop his ass. Here's a little more fuel for your fire, 'You're never a loser until you quit trying!' and 'A trophy carries dust, but memories last forever!' I know, cheesy, right?" Larry rolled his eyes and bobbed his head, laughing.

"You're the best, Larry." I high-fived him.

"I've never seen you quit anything in all the years I have known you." He said with an earnest look. I cocked my head to the side, concerned and puzzled. This wasn't the only time he made like he knew me.

"What do you mean all the years? It's been only four weeks!" I joked.

"Feels like years." He looked nervously at me with a strange smile I'd never seen before. Larry hit me on the shoulder and shoved me towards the court. "Go out there and have fun!"

Greg won the coin toss and chose to serve first. He was already bouncing the ball, preparing his first strike almost before I stepped up to the service line.

Greg yelled over, "You can't stand there."

"Yes, I can," I said back. Greg snarled so loudly I could hear him over twenty yards away.

"It's your loss when I take your head off."

He grunted as he tossed the ball high, hitting a hard serve and expecting to gain his first point. I short-hopped it straight down the line, with no chance for Greg to make a return. I looked at Larry and gave him a big smile—just as we planned and practiced. He really did know what he was talking about.

I refocused as Greg prepared for his second serve. This was no time to get cocky. Greg threw the ball high and served it into the net. He shoved his hand through his hair, wiped the sweat on his shorts, and served again.

I saw it coming and braced myself against the brutal speed. I returned the ball, backpedaling to the baseline of the court. Greg charged the net, and I followed my instruction to deliver a high lob. Greg leaped into the air and smashed the ball like a Wack-A-Mole. So much power and force went into his overhead smash shot that I shivered. This dude would kill me if I let him, but I wouldn't.

"Ha! 15-15. That will keep you on your toes, Max!" Greg taunted. I rolled my eyes, tired of his poking at me. It's good that he's enjoying this, but fun time was over. I got ready to serve for the first time, breathing deeply to get out of my head. I moved myself as far right as possible on the baseline and hit a perfect slice that curved right into the fence before Greg could reach it.

My mother yelled from the stands, "Great serve, Max!"

My next serve was a dink, and Greg took the bait. I loved having so much control using this racquet. I could win this game using this bad boy. During our volley, Greg rushed in and fed me a perfect shot to return to an open court. I jutted my chin toward him and spun my racquet in my hands twice knowing I was on a roll. My next serve was an ace, which really pissed off Greg.

Greg seemed in shock. His eyes scrunched, and his hand went through his hair. A murmur went through the crowd as they watched him get flustered. My skills burrowed under his skin, and he was lost trying to figure out a way to shed me.

A continued feed of noise ran through my head. "Should I open the field of play and give Greg a chance to volley? Would this match be more interesting if I changed up my serves?" I wanted to win, don't get me wrong, but I was bored playing like a robot. I put aside my thoughts for now and stayed the course a while longer.

The match continued until the score read 4-3 in Greg's favor. The crowd cheered and clapped for both of us, hopefully appreciating how hard we both were trying. I could see my mom waving and giving me a thumbs up, but I still didn't see Dad anywhere. That wasn't like him. Usually, he was front and center, trying to coach me. *Did I push him away?*

Instead, Larry yelled at me to call a timeout.

"Max, come over here! I want to give you some mid-match advice." He handed me a water bottle and began his shpiel.

"Greg is picking up on your short hop return of serves. It's time to rotate some new shots into the mix. Change up from staying close to the net to moving back to the baseline. He won't know what you're doing." Larry clapped me on the back, encouraging me along.

"You're doing great! This change of strategy is my last bit of advice. Take him down, Max."

"Larry, I need to use my money shot. Greg keeps giving me an open lane to drill down the line." I pleaded.

"Stick to our plan, only use the money shot for the winning point for the set." Larry's sternness stopped my pleas, I gave him a thumbs-up and went back out to the baseline.

Greg didn't look so good. Some guy was hollering some awful obscenities from the stands. *Was that his dad?* If he was, it was the complete opposite of my parents. If he yelled at me like that, I'd be so embarrassed. Maybe that was the look on his face. I tried to shake my worried feelings away and get my head back in the game.

Five minutes later, Greg was up five games to four. I had to win this, or Greg would blow me out of the water. The next service was mine, I delivered a slice, then a dink, and finished with another ace down the line, bringing the score to 40—love. Greg dug in and returned the next serve, rushing the net as I delivered another perfect high lob. Consistently, Greg delivers another overhead smash, but I don't care because I'm luring him into my game strategy. He thinks he has me on the ropes when, really, I'm about to take him down. One service later, I level up the score, and it's a tie, 5—5. *Don't worry, Greg, I'll put you out of your misery soon.*

We continued to volley while the crowd spun their heads left and right until one of us relented. It was Greg who missed an easy return, bringing our matches to an even 6—6. Tension cut through the air like the stickiness of summer. It was time to hydrate as the sun beat down on us. Unlike the pros, we didn't have umbrellas for shade, clean towels to dry us off, or misting fans to cool us down. No. We were roughing it at summer camp, and the struggle was real.

My mom led the crowd, chanting, "Let's go, Max!" My Happy Hyenas squealed and whistled like a band of wild animals, instilling in me an infectious smile. I was sweating from every pore, but I was still standing and holding strong. I felt grateful to have so many people cheering me on, though an unsettling scene was beginning across the court.

Greg's dad ran from his seat red-faced and grabbed Greg's collar suddenly. "You're embarrassing yourself and me. You're letting this little runt run you all over the court like a carnival clown." He was relentless, but Greg kept his eyes facing down, which made him madder. "Get your act together, idiot, and put this peon back in his place."

My stomach turned, and realization set in. Greg learned to bully from his father. My dad always said you are what you're taught, and Greg learned well. He also learned to hide his shame and weaknesses. *Shit!* That kid had an asshole father he couldn't get away from. From now on, I'll count my blessings, knowing how bad some other kids had it.

Like a sneaky ninja, Larry snuck up on me again, "Max, you're doing fantastic. I'm really proud of you." His praise was lost on me as I shrunk, watching Greg's dad belittling his son in front of everyone.

"Larry. Get Sid. Greg shouldn't have to be treated like that, especially in front of the whole camp. Someone has to do something."

"I will, but you have to snap out of it," Larry pleaded. "Don't let it get to you. We have worked so hard to get to this point to win this match."

I tried to smile and get back in the zone, but the best I could do was our signature double fist pumps.

"You earned this, Max. Finish Greg off, and you can give him a well-deserved monster hug you're so good at.

"Is that really the point of this, Larry? This isn't the summer camp mindset. I don't know if the adrenaline is getting to you, but you have been contradicting yourself this whole week. Winning isn't everything. I need to play well to make everyone happy so they can have good memories of this summer, not how I humiliated another kid.

As it was, Sid walked over to Greg and his dad and directed him off the court with the most disgusted face I'd seen in the three years I'd been coming to Camp Windy City. When the break was over, Sid took his place at center court.

"Please stand and give both these players the recognition they deserve for such a hard-fought battle. Our final game of the match is about to begin, and I don't know about you, but it's anyone's match to win! Finish strong, competitors, and have fun!"

Tiebreaker time. Greg's face was blank, only showing the sweat pouring from his head. His first serve was in, and I returned it with a perfect dink shot across the court. We did the same "dance" as before.

I high-lobbed my return, and Greg used his crushing overhead smash to make his point. No surprise there. However, what did surprise me was the blustering Larry did by calling a timeout.

"Max, you're in a 7-point tiebreaker where every point counts. I don't want to see any more lobs. When and if it comes down to winning your seventh point, I will give you the thumbs up to unleash your money shot." Larry waited for me to agree, but I walked away from him instead.

He didn't understand the spirit of the game and what it meant to Greg if he lost. He needed to make a showing, at least. Nevertheless, I kept going. The tiebreaker went back and forth, and the tension kept building while my desire to win grew less and less. The tiebreaker score was 6—6, and the next point determined the winner. It was decision time.

Larry yelled again, "Show me the money," and gave me the two thumbs up. I was ready to bring home the win when I heard the most awful language from Greg's dad.

"Grrr!" He let out an anguished roar. "What are you doing, you weak-ass pansy?! You're a lumberjack, not a flower girl! Cut that fucking twig down to size!" Greg's dad yelled so loudly everyone in the stands froze, watching my new friend take his father's verbal abuse. Two other fathers tried to calm that asshole down, but the damage to Greg was already done.

Rage rippled off Greg's body and funneled into his serve, which felt more like a cannon. My only option was a short hop to return the ball, creating a vicious volley.

I moved backward and hit another great return Greg delivered from his arsenal of killer shots. Greg retaliated by moving backward and returning another bullet, followed by another wicked shot, including a powerful backhand I hadn't seen up to this point.

I set up a great slice and Greg again returned with a strong forehand. I was exhausted, almost tripping on my own feet, but still managed to hit one of my best underspin shots. It was almost comical how Larry knew exactly what would happen. Greg rushed to the middle of the net and sent a volley back to the baseline, allowing me to counter with my money shot.

This was it, and time stood still. All this training would pay off. I'd be the reigning King of the Campers and have this moment for the rest of my life. When would this ever happen to me again?

I felt the heat pouring down on me and the pressure to please everyone around me. Should I use my double-handed forehand to win the match, or should I help my friend save face?

In a single breath, Larry and I made eye contact, and we both knew my decision. *Sorry, Larry.*

I changed my grip and fed Greg one last perfect high lob, hoping he would hit his powerful overhead smash and win the final point. He needed to win the match more than I did. And when he did, he threw his racquet up in the air.

"YES! Suck it, Dad! In your face! I won!" He yelled out to the heavens as he pumped his elbows behind him, puffing his chest out, doing an odd but joyful victory dance.

Cheers erupted from the crowd to match his enthusiasm, and I walked over and shook his hand. "Tough break, Squirt." He cackled. "It's been fun," and walked back to his bench.

I pressed my lips forward and jutted out my chin. Nothing needed to be said. I made the right decision. He noticed I didn't respond, only jutted his chin towards me as well. From a person who believed me to be an ant beneath his boot four weeks ago, his show of respect now was all I needed. It felt good. Really good. The only thing that could make this better was if...

My suspicions were confirmed when I looked over to Larry, disappointment written all over his face. He sat there with his eyes closed, head lowered, and rubbing his forehead. Deja vu hit me, and for a moment, I saw my dad doing the same thing when he was disappointed with my previous play. Eventually, he stood and walked back up the hill alone. I didn't blame him. Winning this tournament would be another memory Larry and I could share, but for me, it was hanging out together and making memories was what I hoped would be a lifelong friend. My mother waved her hands above her head after she got herself off the bleachers. She ran over and cheered beside my cabinmates, congratulating me on my play and giving Greg a run for his money. *Little did they know.*

"Dude, you were crazy!" Ernie shrieked.

"All that practice paid off, huh?" Dudley said, clapping my back.

"Sad you lost, but insane that you actually stood a chance," Malcom mumbled.

All their compliments and encouragement shored me up after my loss, and it felt good. Mom scanned the crowd, concerned.

"Have you seen your dad? He said he was going to be here, didn't he?"

"Now that you mention it, I looked but couldn't see him during the match. He'll probably show up at some point. There are so many people here that it's almost impossible to see through the crowd.

"If he's here, he's probably sulking about your loss. But, Honey, it didn't really feel like a loss, did it? It was so much fun to watch you enjoy yourself out there with that other boy. I felt really bad about how his father was speaking to him." She brushed my hair from my eyes and stared knowingly into my face.

"That was Greg. My camp rival. Someone who I was scared of but later got to know better."

Several other campers and parents circled around, congratulating me, but my mind was focused on finding my dad. It seemed like forever until a voice rang from the crowd. A familiar voice that told me Dad was over himself and could now face me.

"Max!" My cabinmates split apart like God split the Red Sea. *My dad seemed like a god to me at times, too.* He wasn't dressed impeccably like he usually was, but all I wanted was one of his big bear hugs.

And I didn't have to wait a moment longer. "Hey, Max! I missed you so much, buddy. You were incredible out there." He let me go, and I took a step back, curious.

"Dad, I didn't see you in the stands."

"I was watching from the corner. I was running late and didn't want to force myself into the stands."

"Did you see the whole match?" I asked.

"I saw the whole thing, and you did fantastic." We smiled at each other and I knew instantly he was about to ask if I threw the match.

"I do have one question, though." *Hear the rimshot?* "I saw you had the opportunity to play your money shot and an open lane while Greg was at the net, yet you fed him another perfect lob. Why did you do that?"

I stood tall and said, "I had already proved to myself that I had the confidence and skills to win this challenge. I already had the backing of friends and family cheering me on, no matter if I won or lost. But Greg's dad was so abusive, I knew he needed to win more than I did, and it cost me nothing to let him save face with his father. I already feel like a winner, Dad. I felt it was better to have Greg win because I don't have to come home to a place with that much pressure."

Dad shook his head the way he always did when he had a lightbulb moment. His face was filled with pride and love, his nachas face. Now that I was looking at him closer, I noticed an eerie resemblance of how close it was to Larry's. *Hmm.* He placed a hand on my shoulder, speaking directly to me.

"You're thirteen years old, Max, and already you're a better person and a better man than I will ever be. I am so proud of you." He gave me another great big hug. I remembered the hug I gave Larry. It was the kind my father gave that lifted his spirits, making him feel safe. And, by helping him feel that way, it made me feel safe, too. I guess my dad wasn't so bad after all.

I pulled out of the hug and looked at both Mom and Dad as the rest of the cabin dispersed to meet their own parents.

"Give me a minute. I want to introduce you to Larry." I ran around looking for him.

"Whose Larry?" Dad asked.

"Larry is my new best friend I met here at camp. He helped me kick Greg's butt in football, and then Greg stopped taunting me, sort of. He's the one who showed me a trick to make my arms feel like air when I played basketball and couldn't make a free throw to save my life." I rambled on and on. "Oh, yeah, and so many other things I discovered about myself during the past month. I don't see him around. Maybe he met his parents already?" I looked off to the side and saw Sid. "Hey, Sid! Have you seen Larry?"

Sid shook his head, "Larry came to me and told me he had to go because his ride was here, and they were in a hurry. He said he was sorry he didn't have time to say goodbye, though." That's a bit upsetting. I wanted to thank him and swap phone numbers or something. He probably felt the same way running out of here so fast.

Mom turned to Dad, confused, "Where's your brother? Wasn't he here with you?"

"No. He wanted to get home quickly, so he took off an hour ago." Dad sounded like he was hiding something with every word he spoke. *Would I ever understand him?*

It was party time in the mess hall, and everyone gathered for Duke's best meal of the season, fried chicken. Sid rehashed some of the highlights of the session and encouraged everyone, again, to come back next year. I could be a counselor-in-training, so, maybe—yeah.

"Let's get to the Parent's Day awards!" Sid went on for five minutes, handing out a bunch of visual art awards, their parents' golf clapping after each one. Next were the kayaking awards. Don't ask me how they did it so fast, but there was a two-minute slide show of the various age groups flipping over their boats, trying to get back in, and falling out again. It was hilarious. I hoped someone would send this to *America's Funniest Home Videos*.

"Now it's time for the coveted tennis match winner, Greg Wilson! Congratulations. Please come to the stage." Sid thrust a two-foot trophy with the camp logo on the top as the crowd went nuts cheering Greg as he leapt onto the stage. Sid handed the microphone over to a grateful-looking Greg. *Looks like he finally found some humility.*

"Thank you, everyone, but I want to say that Max really deserves this trophy."

The whole place went silent. This was so uncharacteristic of Greg that even I went wide-eyed. The only one in the room that wasn't shocked was my dad. *What?*

Greg continued. "Max has proven to me and the whole camp that he is a class act. He could have easily won that match. Anyone with eyeballs could see he had the advantage and didn't take it. He looked me straight in the eyes, "You have the heart of a champion, and I have learned a lot from you, so come on up here to get your trophy, friend. But do me a big favor and keep Larry away from me. Pitbull's got a bite!" I grinned and laughed as I walked up on the stage, and the cheers got louder. In my three years here at Camp Windy City, I don't remember Greg being this selfless as he shoved his hand out for me to shake, but I pushed past it and gave him a big, protective hug.

"Dude," he whispered. "Back off. You're freaking me out." Greg handed me the mic, scrubbing at his face in my unexpected show of P.D.A.

"The floor is yours, champ." Not squirt, or runt, or ant—champ. Greg really did come a long way. I wasn't ready to give a speech. However, I knew for a fact that the trophy didn't mean much to me. What mattered was that I made a rival into a good friend. My newfound confidence extended to my cabinmates, and that strengthened our bond even more. I bridged the gap between the misfits and the jocks. It was never about a trophy. So, I took a page from Dad's *Book of Lessons* and began to speak.

"A wise man shared a quote with me, 'A trophy carries dust, but memories last forever!' My prize this season had been all the awesome memories I've made with old and new friends. Anyone who has been to camp knows how cherished these moments are and how important these friends will be for the rest of our lives. Greg, I want you to keep the trophy. Remember our rivalry and our journey to friendship. I know I will." I extended the trophy back towards him, and he took it with glassy eyes. I grabbed his other hand and lifted them between us, and the crowd stood for one last mind-blowing ovation. Knowing smiles were exchanged and we walked off the stage. Dad was beaming, and my mom was dabbing her eyes with a tissue. I hoped he would now understand that I could fend for myself. That I could fall on my own and pick myself up just as quickly. I had confidence in myself I didn't have before summer camp and I knew it shined through.

I'd never *not* need my dad, but today, I felt as strong and confident as he did.

Back in my cabin, I feverishly packed my things. All my attention was given to preparing for my matches, and my stuff was thrown all around my bunk. Honestly, I didn't know if I was packing my stuff or someone else's. As I shoved my toiletry bag into my duffle, I saw a yellow sticky note on my tennis racquet case. I can't believe I missed seeing it until now. *Wait! This isn't my racquet!* I looked for my counselor hoping he could get me Larry's contact information to send this back to him, when I finally read the words on the note. 'Keep the tennis racquet, you earned it. From your best friend, Larry.'

I couldn't tell if I was more shocked by the gift or the bizarre coincidence that Larry's handwriting looked...like my dad's. I rolled the grip of the racquet in my palms when I saw something even more shocking—my dad's initials in small gold capital letters on the bottom edge of the racquet cover. What the hell was going on here? All those coincidences started adding up. Were they coincidences or a cosmic shift? It was time to confront my father about them.

24

MIRACLE FALLOUT

LARRY

I hadn't stuck around after the tennis match, knowing that my time as Larry was over. I didn't know why Max threw the game. Surely, there's no good reason to have done so. I saw that look in his eyes, which told me that there was more to his thoughts than on the surface. I stood up from the floor and zipped my duffle bag and shoved my transformation card in my pocket.

I moved to the mirror on the other side of the cabin and stared at my reflection. I finally got to go to camp and wanted a memory of how I looked before my father's wish ended. I looked calmer than when I got here. I certainly felt more hopeful about my relationship with my son. Max wasn't the only one who grew up at camp this summer. I had so much more respect for my boychic and knew that he knew he didn't need me to fix his life. He only needed me to have my arms open for a bear hug when he needed reassurance. What a wonderful lesson for us both.

I closed my eyes and breathed in and out as I entered into my Zen state of mind. My breath increasingly slowed each time I ran through the cycle. I pulled the card from my pocket, opening it in slow motion Feeling those same tingles ripple through my body, and I thanked God and Dad for the opportunity to be with Max as a peer. One second, I was a small, stocky replica of my thirteen-year-old self, and the next. . .I opened my eyes, hoping to be a better-fit version of my previous self, *after all, I'd been exercising like an animal for a month*, to a paunchy middle-aged man with a head full of black hair stuffed into a tiny, over-stretched red t-shirt. I laughed at myself in this pathetic-looking shirt and pulled it off carefully. *This was coming home with me.* I tucked the worn shirt under the other clothes shoved in my bag and grabbed my other duffle with the adult clothes from when I made my transformation at the gas station. The idea of leaving my prized T2000 was an easy one. It would blow Max's mind to have this powerhouse forever, and I could watch him continue working on his game with the memories it conjured up.

There was little talking on the way home, unlike our usual banter after camp. Ilene focused on the road, but Max seemed all broody. I hoped it was only tiredness from training, the sun, and his match. I still mulled over how I felt about Max throwing his championship game and my time with Max as Larry.

Ilene called her sister-in-law, and that would last about five hours, minimum. Minimum because she was a card-carrying subscriber to the School of Creative Driving. It didn't matter that she had a navigation system on her car; she wasn't going to "relinquish her freedom" to technology. It was a small price to pay to relax and get some shut-eye.

In and out of consciousness, I overheard her asking, "Do I hear Dale in the background?"

"Yes, of course." Her sister-in-law responded.

"Out of curiosity, how long has he been home?" Ilene asked.

"All day."

I didn't need to open my eyes to know Ilene was also looking at me, probably very annoyed. I might add that she poked me in the leg, not so nicely, engaging her attorney-mode. Her investigative voice asked, "How did your brother drop you off an hour ago when he's been home all day?"

Good question. "I'm exhausted. Let's discuss it later." I turned my body toward the window. How do I tell her that the wish I made came true?

My wife, who never growls, growled. "I'm sure it will be a *magical* tale." I'm pretty sure she's on to me, but there's no way she would believe that it actually happened, right? Even Dale couldn't believe it until he saw me as Larry. Max huffed. Was he listening to our conversation?

"Why did he leave without saying goodbye? What does Larry have to do with Dad?" These were a lot of questions I hadn't planned for. My world was caving in, and I needed an escape route—fast!

"Hmm?" I looked back at him.

"Nothing. It's just that I think I told you earlier about how I met a kid named Larry. He was new to Camp Windy City, and we really hit it off. We did everything together, almost like we were attached at the hip. It was so easy to talk about any subject, and we would have fun in whatever we did together."

Ilene gave me a conspiratorial look, then turned her head forward. "That sounds like the relationship you have with your father."

"Is it?" I mumbled. I'm still not sure if Max reciprocated that thought. "Did you learn to ride a bike at camp?" I sighed, knowing that was something he and Larry never did. Perhaps that would throw him off the trail.

Max looked up at me from his stupor, having heard my question. "No. I guess I will go through life without ever knowing how to ride a bike." His sarcasm told the whole story. "And I know how that disappoints you so much that I prefer rollerblading."

He cocked his head to the side, indicating he wasn't letting go of this whole Larry is Dad thing. I need more time to come up with a plan.

I sat back, defeated. "Let's spend these next few more hours enjoying the scenery or napping. Not you, Ilene. You keep driving safely." We all chuckled. If the truth can set you free, then I'm a dead man in chains trying to spin this with my wife and kid. My only saving grace was that I had told her about my dream; Dale, too. The fact that I had a magical transformation was way beyond sane reasoning, and I'm pretty sure I had lost my mind thinking I'd go through with all of this and come out Scott-free. I'd find a way to iron this out with my wife. Max, unfortunately, was a whole other matter. I'd made up my mind to get Ilene on board first, and together, we could talk to Max. He was going to be so pissed off.

"What's going on with you and your son?" Ilene's accusing tone pushed my internal buttons.

"Nothing I can't handle. Give me some space and time, and I will take care of everything." I lied to myself, putting my head back in the sand.

A few more days passed and the relationship with my son was akin to the Alaskan tundra in December—frigid. Ironically, it was the middle of summer, and no one had called me out on my deception. The question of who would speak first was still up for grabs, and I was still being an ass and now owning my story. I wanted to clear the air. I really did. It was on the tip of my tongue. I revved up to tell my family what I had done when Max got a call from Ernie and Malcolm saying they were coming to play video games. My story would take more than an hour to tell and dissect, so again, I laid low.

"Max, get Larry on a conference call with the rest of the guys. He's the only one not playing. This would be epic!" Ernie whooped, punching the air.

After hanging around outside, I came in for lunch and overheard the kids playing in my den. *Oh, shit!*

I positioned myself so I could see what was going on in the room through the reflection of the dining room mirror without being detected.

Ernie held up a picture for everyone to see. "Remember this one?"

Everyone on the call laughed, and Walter's eyebrows raised from his square on the screen.

"That's the basketball shot of the century." Walter reminisced. "Max shot a swish from half-court. It was insane! We were so hyped, remember Max?" Max seemed lost in thought, and his friends kept looking at him. Why wasn't he engaging with his friends?

"Who took this picture?" Max said, accusingly grabbing the picture from Ernie's hand.

Malcolm responded, confused. "What picture? They took a picture?"

Dudley spoke from his corner of the screen, "I did, why?"

"Don't you remember Larry very strongly said, 'No pictures of him, ever!'" Max shouted.

These kids were smart. If they pieced together that I was Larry and Larry was me, I'd ruin my kids' life forever. As they passed around the picture and held it up to the camera for the other boys to see, I panicked—my t-shirt!

I bolted from my hiding place and ran upstairs, searching for that damn shirt I squirreled away. Did Ilene see it? Did she wash it? Hide it? Where the hell was it?

I heard Ilene cross the marble foyer heading for the den. Noo!

"That's from the football game, and it was a group picture after we won," Malcolm said, handing the picture to Ilene. She always brought snacks to Max's friends, so why would today be any different? *Argh!*

"I don't remember Dudley taking that picture, but apparently, he did." I grabbed the clothes from the laundry basket, then snuck down the stairs, carrying them as my excuse for being around, and flicked on the intercom from the laundry room. Finally, I could hear everything they said clearly.

"A nice-looking bunch of boys?" she asked as she admired the photo, unaware of the discrepancy.

"Sure. But take a look at that kid." Max grabbed more pictures from the shelf. "Here we are at the lake, the mess hall, and all of us at the campfire with s'mores. There were a lot of good moments. Larry, the guy I told you about who was my best friend, was explicit about not photographing him but there he is, again, while we were playing football."

Ilene looked over the photos while Max continued to talk. "Larry was amazing. He was a kid who always had my back. He always did things with me no matter how much grief we gave each other about it. We were like Siamese twins, except for the tremendous size difference." He laughed at his wry humor.

"Which one of you boys specializes in Photoshop?" I could feel dread heavy on my body.

Max questioned her, "What do you mean?"

"Well, you said this is a picture of your friend, Larry, but in truth, that's a picture of your dad when he was probably thirteen years old."

"You're crazy, Mom." I heard Max hit the floor hard. "That's Larry, his full name is Larry Pit."

"I don't know who is playing a trick on you, but if you look closely, you can see the boy in this picture is wearing his favorite red Pitbull shirt. Which one of you stinkers is playing a prank on my son?

"Listen, guys, do you mind calling it quits today? I need to think. We can meet up again tomorrow." Max said, dejectedly. The sound of the front door opening and closing was my cue to cut the intercom and focus on the laundry. *Hoo-boy.* This shit was getting pretty thick around here.

I loaded the washing machine and left the laundry room, scurrying back to my hiding place.

"It can't be true. No way." Max said, still denying what Ilene was saying.

"I can prove it if you like."

Ilene gestured for Max to follow her across the room to my bookshelves. She searched through the albums and showed Max a picture of me wearing the same red T-shirt with "Pitbull" on it when I played pee wee football in my youth.

"See the resemblance? The name "Larry Pit" alone is a giveaway. Your father's middle name is Lawrence, and Larry is short for Lawrence. His favorite shirt and nickname were Pitbull."

Ilene swayed and dropped into a chair, clinging the album to her chest. It appeared she had put all those pieces together. She's way too good for me and my espionage.

"Max, don't you find it coincidental that your new best friend's name is Larry Pit?"

"I don't know. There were signs at camp. Is Dad Larry? It's crazy and impossible. This is a shitty joke." Max bellowed, his arm flailing around him as he stomped around the room. I understood firsthand how incomprehensible this situation was. It would take time for it all to make sense.

Ilene stopped Max as he made to leave the room. "Someone has played a cruel joke on you, and I don't know why. I'll help you figure it out." She reached out, touching his arm. "This seems like a job for an attorney, right?"

"If anyone can figure this out, it's you, Mom." He kissed her cheek, left the room, and climbed the stairs just in time for my getaway.

I slipped from my hiding place and out to the garage unnoticed, or so I thought. I walked about five feet into the garage and heard the door open behind me.

Ilene demanded, "Who, why, and what does Larry Pit have to do with you or anyone you know?"

I acted surprised and turned, "What happened?"

"Max is very confused about some camp pictures one of the boys brought over. Max showed me the picture of his new best friend, Larry, and I told him someone had been very creative with the picture. Why, might you ask? Because you are wearing your lucky Pitbull jersey. Care to share, Howard?"

I sighed. I was busted, and Ilene was pissed off. Not a good combination. I'd only once seen her this way, and that was when she was about to deliver Max. I told her

I had a work thing, and she threatened to castrate me. Never again! I walked back into the house and plopped down at the kitchen table for that long talk I'd been putting off.

"I know I have a lot of explaining to do, but I am not sure where to start."

"Let's start from the end. How did your brother drop you off at the camp when he was actually home all day with his family? And don't leave out any details."

I straightened my posture and tried my best to act like a defense attorney, but after a few minutes of silence and wringing my hands together, I blurted out, "You won't believe any of this, so I am just going to tell you the truth. I never went on a golf trip. Instead, I became thirteen years old again. I was at camp for the whole month trying to teach Max everything I could that I couldn't teach him as his father." I felt light-headed and out of breath. I was afraid that all this disclosure might give me a heart attack.

Ilene sat down, smiling at me in the most unsettling way possible.

"I know you are a good liar, Howard. And I remember your whole crazy magical epiphany two months ago, but this one takes the cake." She patted my hand and stood to get herself a glass of water.

"When you're ready to tell me the truth, you know where to find me. If not for me, then for Max." Ilene left the garage, leaving me to stew in my own thoughts.

There was only one good place to do that—in my comfy chair.

Max, having probably heard the garage door open and close and more footsteps leaving the kitchen, stormed downstairs into the den to confront me. I was ready for him to tell me I was crazy. That is impossible. That he would never trust me again. What could I tell him that would make him believe me? The truth. I would tell him the truth, but more likely, he'd leave like his mother.

Like a frigid gust of wind, Max lit into me.

"Who was Larry? Why did you hire a kid to become my best friend, mentor me, and teach me all the things you thought I had to know? Why did you do this to me?"

He needed the truth, and I would treat him like a man as I did it. He was old enough to understand my desperation and the mystical nature of the universe. God knows I'd beaten it into him since he could talk.

"Before this gets out of hand, the truth is, I am and was Larry." His silence was deafening. Max struggled to deny what happened at camp and his reality today. I don't blame him. My miracle was unexplainable.

Max asked again, "Why and who did you hire to be Larry Pit?"

"No one. Please give me a few minutes to walk you through this, okay?" My hands were pressed together, begging him to open his heart and mind to my tale.

"Think about it for a minute," I said to Max. "Larry and I have so many characteristics in common because we were the same person. I didn't go on a golf trip. Instead, I magically became thirteen again and came to your camp to become your best friend. And I can prove it."

I pulled up the footage from the doorbell-cam on the night of my birthday dinner to show Max the guy who delivered my birthday package. "Also, you can ask your Uncle Dale, he was in on it as well. Please believe me. I am and was Larry." I whispered.

Max screamed back, "You're a liar! I'm never speaking to you again!" He turned and rushed up the stairs, yelling the same thing repeatedly.

It wasn't long before Ilene opened the now-closed door to the den. I slumped over in my chair, pathetic. I looked at her helplessly, "I would never lie to you and Max, and one day, you'll understand I'm not lying to either of you. I needed to do this."

"You sound delirious, so let's call it a day and figure this out another time." Her generous nature was precisely what I needed at that moment. I took her hand, and we walked up to bed together.

Days go by, and I'm still trying to convince Ilene and Max that I wasn't lying. Newsflash: It wasn't working. We walked past each other without a "Good morning"

or even acknowledging we were in the same house. It's painful. If I couldn't convince them, I'd try to distract myself by learning to rollerblade. I hopped in the car, headed for the sporting goods store to purchase my rollerblades, and enjoyed this beautiful day. Besides, sitting in my house was the last thing I wanted to do.

When I returned, Ilene was there waiting with an exasperated look on her face. *What now?*

"What's all this?"

"Oh, these are my new rollerblades," I said, smiling.

"What do you think you are doing with those? I stood up, balancing myself against one of the cars in the garage.

"Max has gone on and on about how great rollerblading was, and I figured why not join him. If you excuse me, I've got to get some practice in. Especially if we get to see some FTBs when we're out there."

"What the hell are FTBs?" Ilene snapped back, confused.

I exploded in laughter "Full Titty Bras. If you want to stay up with your son, you'll learn the lingo. Max taught me that at camp."

Her face went dark, "That's disgusting."

"Yeah, well, it came out of our son's mouth. Gotta love him." I grinned. "Don't worry, it'll be good to learn how to do something that he likes so we can spend time together on his terms."

"If it gets you closer to telling us the truth, I won't stop you."

"At camp, Max told me that he didn't like riding bikes but loved rollerblading. I never taught him, so he never knew if he liked it. I felt like a horrible father. Hence, the blades." I said, pointing to my feet.

"You and your flights of fancy." She shook her head, "Stay safe!"

"I'll try!" I shouted back as I began to walk-skate hesitantly out of the garage. I expected to be wobbly at the start. The store clerk insisted I get a helmet and elbow and knee pads. I passed on the helmet because I already had one for biking, but like an idiot, I was stubborn and foolish and didn't put it on when I left the garage later that afternoon. After I almost killed myself on the uneven sidewalk, I hit the street. That came with its own set of problems—hills. In retrospect, I should have taken the advice of wearing a helmet as I went barreling down, unable to stop. My feet swung out under me, and my body spun into the air; I crashed to the ground with a heavy splat as my head hit the pavement.

25

HEARTBROKEN

ILENE

Sirens zoomed past my windows while I did the dishes. "Poor soul." I didn't think much of it because they go by all the time.

I couldn't understand those things Howard had been saying recently. Why would Howard lie like that? Why would he hire someone to be Max's friend? Is he really telling the truth? The signs were there, sure, but it's way too unbelievable to be a reality. I remembered that night when he had that weird dream. Something about wishes, his dad, and spending more time with Max as a peer. None of it made sense. I shook my head and went outside, walking down my driveway, wondering how close those firetrucks were. I could see the tops of their rigs and kept walking up the hill until I reached the top. *Oh my god! Howard!!*

I raced over to the firemen, begging them to let me through.

"That's my husband! Howard! I'm here." I screamed hysterically.

My neighbor caught me by the elbow and told me she was drinking her coffee in the kitchen when she saw Howard fall and hit his head. She called 9-1-1 and waited by his side until they arrived. I thanked my lucky stars that someone saw what happened. He could have been alone, dying on the road, maybe even dead.

The EMTs patched him up enough to get him on a gurney while I looked on in horror. My wonderful Howard went to the ends of the earth to connect with his son and almost killed himself doing it.

"Ma'am. Would you like to ride with your husband to the hospital?" *I do, but. . .Max.*

"I need to tell my son. He's home alone. I'll follow behind in a few minutes."

He gave me the information on a business card, and I called Karen, Dale, and Al while I ran home.

I burst through the front door, yelling to Max, frantic. "Max! Dad got into a horrible accident. I must go to the hospital. Your aunt and uncles will wait with you. They will be here in a few minutes. I need to go now to be with him. Be brave, sweetheart. I'll call you as soon as I know something." I grabbed my purse and checked for my keys.

"Wait! Let me come with you, please!" My son may have been thirteen, but he looked like he was five years old, shaking in fear.

I was so choked up my voice cracked.

"I know you do. Please stay home with your uncles and aunt. I am sure it's going to be a long night, and I need to rush to the hospital now. Everything will be fine, I promise."

He rushed down the stairs to hug me, though I think it was more for him. "At least tell me what happened. What kind of accident? Is it really bad? Don't leave me with nothing!"

I calmed myself enough to get the words out clearly. Max had never seen me react so erratically before. It made sense that he was this worried.

"Max, all I know is your dad fell while he was trying to rollerblade. He hit his head when he fell and broke his arm while trying to break his fall." Everything was happening so fast. I needed to get to the hospital and hoped that was enough for my son to let me go.

Max placed his hands on my shoulders, looking directly at my eyes. "How do you know he was rollerblading?" His voice was trembling.

"I saw your dad trying to sneak out of the house with his new rollerblades, and when I confronted him, his only response was, 'I want to learn and blade with my son and hopefully see some FTBs.' He headed down the sidewalk, and the next thing I heard were the sirens. I had a weird feeling and went out to check what house they were at. By the time I came over the hill, he was on a stretcher, and the paramedics were there to let me know about the accident."

"Please, take me with you." Max pleaded again.

"Max, I love you, but this is not the time to argue with me."

"Max, you are staying home for now. I need to go to him." I said, calmly.

"How bad is Dad? Will he be okay?" Max asked, increasingly concerned as his voice rose until he realized he was yelling. He calmed down before mumbling, "It's all my fault, isn't it?"

"Don't be silly," and hugged him tightly. "Let me go, and I am sure everything will be fine. I want you to call me once your uncles and aunt get here, and I will call as soon as I know more details."

I kissed his forehead and hustled to the car.

26

REALIZATION

MAX

U ncle Dale, Uncle Al, and Aunt Karen arrived a few minutes after Mom left, asking me a million questions I couldn't answer. I couldn't take it anymore and went upstairs to my room. I could still hear them chattering to each other as they huddled at the bottom of the staircase. Moments later, I heard a knock at my bedroom door. I pulled myself out of bed and opened the door to my Aunt Karen, worry written all over her face.

"Max!" Aunt Karen whisper-yelled, pulling me into a big hug. "Please come downstairs and sit with us. You must be so shaken up about your dad. I'll even make you a milkshake if it would make you happy." *You can't say no to Aunt Karen—and a milkshake.*

My aunt got busy fulfilling her promise, "What happened?" she asked, removing the chocolate ice cream from the freezer.

"What do you know?" Uncle Al followed up.

My heart felt tight, and my head spun with so many known and unknown feelings zipping through me. My mind stopped on the word regret. Was this my fault? Why didn't I give him a chance to explain everything before running away like a brat? I took a deep breath, trying to settle myself down. I needed to figure out my emotions and I couldn't do it flipping out.

"Look, all I know is Dad got hurt while he was rollerblading."

"Rollerblading?" Uncle Dale questioned, "He would never get off four wheels, except when he would ride his bike. Do you know why he would be so foolish to try that?"

"I have some idea, but I still don't believe it happened." I looked down at the table, not understanding why I felt guilty about something that wasn't real.

Uncle Dale asked again, more aggressively, "What could you have said or done to make him do something so foolish?" My head was pounding, and I slumped in my chair, all eyes on me.

I mumbled, "Dad said he was Larry," waving the comment off. Dad loved to weave stories. This had to be another work of fiction.

Uncle Dale suddenly pulled back and took a deep breath. He looked at us as if trying to decide whether to tell us something. *Does he know about Larry?*

In unison, Uncle Al and Aunt Karen asked, "Who's Larry?" Just then, the phone rang.

Uncle Dale answered the phone and immediately put it on speaker because Mom was on the line.

"I have an update."

Her voice hiccupped as she spoke, and we could hear the pain in her voice. "The doctors are examining Howard now. His broken arm is set, but his head injury has the staff concerned. They recommended that, with all the swelling they saw, he be put into a drug-induced coma so that his body could heal faster. This is all too much!" She bawled into the phone and then recovered soon after sighing. "We won't know anything for a while. Please pray for a miracle." She hiccupped again, and we all replied in unison, 'Of course we will.'

"Is Max there? I need to hear his voice."

I didn't hesitate. "I'm here, Mom. Can I come and sit with you now? I don't want to leave you alone."

For the first time since hearing about my dad's accident, I broke down crying.

"Oh, baby. Don't cry. Dad will be okay. It's best if you stay home for now. Knowing you're with family is enough for me. I want you to stay calm and for everyone to get some rest if you can. I'll be all right."

She tried to say all this with conviction, but I wasn't buying it.

"Okay, Mom. But I'm coming over first thing in the morning. Even if I need to take a ride share." I walked away from the call and began to pace around the kitchen table.

"Thanks for letting us know," Uncle Dale said softly. "Get some rest yourself when you can. He wouldn't want you to hurt yourself for his sake."

"Right." She agreed, and we could hear her breaking down before she could hang up. It was quiet momentarily as we all sat in dread and worry. Uncle Dale looked at me, probably trying to make heads or tails of what I said.

He stared me down and asked again, "Did you say something to your dad to get him to try rollerblading? I'm sure you told him more than you thought. Call me a liar if you want, but your dad pulled off a miracle to get to know you better."

What? What did that mean? Is he insinuating what I think he is? Was Uncle Dale a part of this mystery?

Uncle Dale closed his eyes and shook his head. After a long sigh, he looked out the window, deep in thought.

"It's getting late, and we can only pray and hope for the best. Max, try to get some rest. We'll be down here if your mom calls with any news. I'll get you myself as soon as we know something. Promise."

I opened my mouth to say something but shut it just as fast. It had been a really long day, so I didn't even realize how tired I was. I was about to fall asleep when I overheard their conversation outside on the driveway.

"What the fuck is happening?" Aunt Karen accused Uncle Dale.

"Who the hell is Larry?" Uncle Al blustered.

"What miracle are you speaking of?" Karen swiped back for another go at Uncle Dale.

Talk about an interrogation. These two weren't even trying to play good cop/bad cop. I was happy because I had the same questions and was tired of waiting for an answer.

I exited my bed, cracked the window, and slid to the floor. I wanted to hear every detail. Not some watered-down version later.

In one quick breath, though, Uncle Dale spilled the beans in one long-winded explanation.

"All right already. You won't believe me, but don't interrupt until I'm done. "Howard did his meditation thing where he reached out to Dad to turn back time and become thirteen years old again to be with Max for four weeks at summer camp. Dad apparently agreed and delivered a package with a card the night of his birthday. You won't believe me even if I show you the doorbell video for proof. I drove him to camp, and he opened his birthday card again. In a split second, Howard turned back into his thirteen-year-old body and called himself Larry. That's it, end of story."

Their voices quieted, so I kneeled to peer out the window. Uncle Dale sat on the big rock beside the driveway, staring at his siblings. Aunt Karen stared into space, speechless, until Uncle Al burst into laughter.

"Wow, Dale! That was quite a story. Props to you for your creativity. Now, come on, man, give us the truth." I listened in as I continued watching from my window.

Uncle Dale reached into his pocket and pulled out his phone.

"I am not supposed to do this, but I have proof. I have a picture of him when he became Larry." He held up his phone for everyone to see. *Damn! I'm too far away!*

"Who's that kid getting into your truck, Dale? Uncle Al pointed to the phone.

"That's our brother when he was about thirteen years old!" Both Karen and Dale blurt out together.

Dale continued. "Yes, it is. But I took that picture over a month ago when I dropped him off at Camp Windy City."

"Oh. My. God. Does Ilene or Max know?" Aunt Karen asked incredulously.

"Ilene knows nothing, but I think Max has started puzzling it all together." Uncle Dale swiped across his screen and played the video of Dad's package being delivered. Did he do it to validate what he said? I don't know. I knew Dad tried to tell me about this magical fantasy thing, and I blew him off. Magical wishes weren't something I could take seriously. I thought he was hiding something sinister, like being a secret agent or a Russian spy. I'd never have dreamed his meditation exercise was so powerful that it could change an adult to being a kid.

I locked the window, slipping back into bed to stare at my ceiling as I imagined a projector screen up there. All the images from camp flowed out on the screen, and I began a meditation routine, picturing every moment I spent with Larry. How many thirteen-year-old boys shared so many inspirational quotes? Uncle Dale's comments also match Larry's, saying he never rollerbladed, for he was more of a roller-skate kid. Larry's commanding personality, hatred for bullies, fear of heights, and comments like, "All the years I have known you" played on a loop.

And his tennis racquet, the T2000? I even remembered Larry's response when I told him my dad had a similar racquet in the attic. He mentioned Jimmy Connors, a person who I had no idea about, but my dad was old enough to remember that guy. What about all those movie quotes? I am the movie quote guy, but Larry leaned down to help me after he pushed me to the ground and said, "Luke, I am your father." There were so many signs, though I had never put them together because it was impossible! But the one piece I couldn't ignore was the piece of the red Pitbull shirt.

I jumped up, yanked open the nightstand drawer, and pulled out the piece of fabric I had torn from Larry's shirt. Dad said he had some clothes he needed to wash yesterday, and I rushed down to the laundry room before my family came back into the house.

I opened the washer, but it was empty. The dryer, however, was full I searched through all the clothes and miraculously found the red shirt—big letters of Pitbull unmistakably on the front and a torn piece missing at the hem.

I spread out the shirt and pieced together my souvenir and almost fainted. There it was. It's a perfect fit. Like goddamn Cinderella, it was a perfect fit. Dad wasn't lying. Dad was Larry, and Larry was Dad. I placed the ripped piece of shirt on top of the Pitbull shirt on the dryer and headed back upstairs in hopes of falling asleep. Maybe my dreams will answer the rest of my questions, like how could my dad physically make this transformation? I don't know. Nothing made sense at the moment. Dad was given a magic miracle that had thrown all earthly logic out the window. What's a kid to do with that information?

27

THE BOYCHIC

MAX

It was late, and I couldn't fall asleep for the life of me. I was exhausted and hungry from missing dinner but couldn't get myself out of bed. Sleep took over as I remembered the last things I saw on the side table of Dad's den: some magazines and a cassette player. A few hours passed when I woke up as the sun rose. My stomach churned and creaked, begging for food, and I gave up trying to sleep any longer. I snuck downstairs, not to wake anyone, and decided to bypass the kitchen for the laundry room. I needed to see that shirt again and figure out how this whole story went together. Any thoughts about becoming a ninja were squashed when I heard a soft voice behind me.

"Max?" The voice of Uncle Dale, who probably struggled to sleep like myself, stood in the doorframe with a sly grin. "Trouble sleeping?" I nodded and pointed a finger at the shirt lying on the washer.

"Holy shit! Come on, Boychic. It's time we have a little talk." He threw his arm over my shoulder and walked me into the den, closing the door behind him.

I went to speak, but he cut me off.

"Your dad wasn't lying. He really was Larry!" I rubbed my eyes with the palms of my hands, clearing a path of acceptance for his words. It had to be possible. The proof was in front of my eyes.

"How did that even happen?" I left my hands on my face as Uncle Dale pulled up the rolling chair alongside me and leaned back.

"Let's start with your dad's birthday party," he said calmly. "Do you remember when you opened the door and received a package?" I nodded slowly.

I re-watched the doorbell video and almost fell over. It wasn't just some guy, but my dad, your grandfather, gave you the gift for Howard. The transaction was so quick you never would have registered it as him, especially since he passed when you were only a baby. As quickly as he came, he vanished into thin air seconds after you closed the door." He breathed and then asked, "Have you ever heard the word Boychic mentioned by your father?"

"Of course! He uses it whenever he gets the chance. Come to think of it, even Larry said that to me before the tennis match. He blew it off, but it stayed with me. What exactly does it mean?"

Uncle Dale leaned forward. "A Boychic is a strong bond between child and parent. It's a term of endearment. Your dad had the same relationship with his dad. They could feel each other's emotions and sometimes even their thoughts. They did everything together. They could feel each other's happiness or sadness like a sympathetic vibration. Howard tried to explain all of this when our father passed away. He was emphatic that he had felt our dad reach out to him with a final hug as he took his last breath. The look on his face was eerie, yet he was grateful when he explained it."

"That's intense." I stuttered, and Uncle Dale put his hands on my knees.

"It is. Deep in his heart, I know you are Howard's Boychic, but only you can sense that." He said, with a confident and knowing smile.

"I don't know how to sense that!" I cried. What was I supposed to do with all this information? Did Uncle Dale think I could mind-meld myself with my dad and fix him? Was I the reason all this wacky stuff happened? I couldn't get my head around it.

"I think you do."

"How?"

"Howard always told me if he felt he needed dad around, he would do his meditation routine. When he was young, he called it fantasy traveling. I thought he was nuts. I never made time to do it after your grandpa took me through a few times. Your dad was the master, and I know that he not only showed you but practiced it with you as soon as you could walk. Would you be a sport and remind me how it's done? It may be the only way we'll get some answers to our questions."

"All right," I said, moving into my dad's chair.

Uncle Dale got up and turned on the small desk lamp next to the big, comfy chair, illuminating what was on the table. I saw two magazines, Boy's Life and Chicago, which he loved to read whenever he wasn't focused on work, sports, or myself. He also kept a cassette player on the table, though I didn't understand why.

"Your dad hated listening to any music. Why would he have a cassette player?"

"He told me he listened to a particular song while he spent his final hours with his dad during hospice."

"What the hell?" He jumped up and paced back and forth a few times, then sat down with a thump.

"That's so weird. Let's come back to that. Now, show me how you got into your relaxed state of mind."

"Okay. It goes like this. I sit in the chair, close my eyes, and visualize a powder blue sky with giant white fluffy clouds. Then I visualize a big white balloon in front of my face. I inhaled, blowing out as hard as possible, and pushing the balloon with my breath. Dad said to repeat the sequence ten times. The first time I saw the balloon clearly. By the fifth time, the balloon became faint. And by the eighth time, the balloon would disappear into the clouds. By the time I got to ten, my breathing would be very calm and deep, and my whole body and mind would be fully relaxed.

Uncle Dale pursed his lips and nodded. "Okay, I think I understand. Would you demonstrate this for me now?"

"Why?" I wondered. What was he getting at?

"Trust me. I have a hunch."

"Fine, but I'm warning you. I haven't done it entirely in months. I jumped up, shook my arms and legs, then plopped down again, trying to take this seriously.

Inhale. Exhale. Repeat.

There's the balloon. I inhaled again and gently blew the balloon away. *Boychic. The magazines.* That word and image kept repeating. I continued the fantasy traveling ritual that Dad taught me. *Boychic.* Again, why? I fidgeted in the chair uncomfortably.

Uncle Dale broke my concentration, "I thought this was supposed to calm you, but from the look of things, it's anything but. You look uncomfortable and nervous, and you're sweating. What's wrong?"

I opened my eyes and stopped the breathing technique. *Boychic.* Gah! There was a message here, but I couldn't figure it out.

"I keep hearing that word in my head!" I whined. I stood up, angry, confused, and scared. I pointed to the magazines in front of me.

"I keep seeing these magazines in my mind. I don't know what any of this means. I need to stop. I don't want to do this anymore!"

Without thinking, I stood abruptly and flipped the side table over. I instinctively reached to the side and, with one swipe, heaved it into the wall. The bulb on the lamp shattered as it hit the ground, and those magazines flew behind me. The only thing I saw during my fit was the cassette player flying over to the side and opening up mid-flight.

"Relax," Uncle Dale yelled. I stared across the room at no particular thing as I regained my control. The room was silent. I dropped to my knees and held them to my chest, wrapping my arms tightly around them. I hung my head and cried. I was a shit son. I pushed Dad away when I knew all he wanted was the best for me. Why couldn't I let him do his thing and not always be annoyed?

"Hey, bud..." Uncle Dale knelt before me and placed his hands on my shoulders. Let's pick this stuff up and rest. I had no idea how much pain this exercise was doing to you. I'll let it go." He helped me up, and we went to work putting things back the best we could.

Uncle Dale reached for the magazines, and his eyes widened. I carefully stepped over the broken glass to see what caught his attention. *Oh my God.* The magazines fell against the wall under the window, awkwardly falling over each other to reveal the word "Boychic." As the daylight illuminated the word, a shiver ran through my body, followed by a warm pulse traveling from my head to my feet. I looked at Uncle Dale in awe of this feeling and settled into its warmth.

"Oh, my God!" Uncle Dale gasped. "Your dad is reaching out to you."

What? I looked at him, confused and worried. A spark of something I needed began to flicker and reawaken in me—hope. This was something Larry ingrained into me at camp.

28

BACK FROM THE DEAD

MAX

U ncle Dale and I ran out of the den, me holding the magazines. We surprised Uncle Al and Aunt Karen in the kitchen while they were drinking coffee. I'm sure I woke them up when I threw the table. Everything happened so fast afterward it didn't occur to me that I would wake them up.

I had opened my mouth to deliver a convincing excuse for making so much noise when Mom walked into the house, exhausted and disheveled. As she removed her coat, Uncle Dale rushed over and pushed it back on.

"Everyone, get in the car. We need to get to the hospital ASAP!" Everyone was in their pajamas but ran for their shoes, screaming, "Why?" "What's going on?" "Is it Howard?"

Dale reassured everyone, "I will explain everything on the way to the hospital. Ilene, give me your keys. You're in no shape to drive."

If I had been a bystander, it would have looked like a hectic scene from a *Home Alone* movie. We hustled out of the house and ran around Mom's car, trying to find an open seat. Uncle Dale had his seatbelt on before anyone was in the car and began driving away as the doors slammed shut. I'm squished between family members but still gripping tightly onto the two magazines. My insides still felt warm, and my connection to Dad was fading.

Uncle Dale stared straight ahead as he rushed into his explanation.

"You should know that I was a part of Howard's plan to change into a thirteen-year-old. I knew weeks before his scheme and thought I'd humor him. But when I tell you, he hopped into my truck looking exactly like Howard when we were kids. I almost choked on my saliva."

He went on. "Ilene, you remember the night Howard had his crazy dream? You know, the one with the miracle and wishes and our dad?" He waited for her to catch up on his remarks.

Awareness dawned on her face. "That was the craziest thing. He was so sure his dad would come to him in a dream. Who was I to question him? Things like that happen all the time."

It sounded like she was talking herself into believing the beginnings of this rollercoaster story.

"He only told you half the story. He didn't want to worry you." Mom looked like she would throttle my uncle for not telling her later.

"Your husband asked our dad to perform a miracle to help Howard turn back into his thirteen-year-old self. Howard felt he was losing his son, so he thought this was his best chance to become a peer rather than his stubborn old self as his father. He thought if he joined Max at camp, it would bring them closer together."

Aunt Karen lost it. "That has to be the stupidest thing I've ever heard. It's not possible." She threw herself back against her seat, knocking me into Uncle Al.

"I know. It's ridiculous, but like I said, I helped him with the logistics, and when he transformed into this kid, I became a believer. The plan was Howard would be Larry for the thirty days at Camp Windy City, and when camp was over, he would return to Howard. Of course, there are few more details, but this is the gist of the story."

He stopped at a red light and pulled up a picture on his phone of Larry to show Mom. We all leaned forward to take a peek, and we all gasped. It really was him.

"That's my friend, Larry," I said, dazed and confused. Mom, however, stared at the picture for a long time, emotionless and distracted.

Uncle Dale continued. "Let's skip forward. I had Max show me how he did the meditation thing Howard does. I saw he was the opposite of calm from the meditation, screaming that he kept hearing a whisper of a word he couldn't understand and that he kept seeing the two magazines in his head. You know, the ones that have been sitting at his side table for twenty years? When Max got flustered, threw the table over, and everything fell to the floor. But get this: those magazines Max holds now are spelled boychic when overlapped."

I interrupted, holding up the magazines precisely as he described them so Mom, Aunt Karen, and Uncle Al could see.

"See? The magazines' titles spell out *Boychic*." My enthusiasm met with disbelief. "I. Am. His Boychic." I hollered every word. He had called me. I could feel him, sense him."

Our conversation halted as we pulled into the hospital parking lot. Every door flew open before Uncle Dale had put the car in Park. Mom ran ahead without checking in with reception, directing us to Dad's room. Dad was hooked up to all kinds of machines where monitors beeped and blipped. The room was cold and sterile, and it felt like dread. My head spun when I finally focused on my dad's face. The tube down his throat and more tubes stuck into his arms looked like an alien had invaded his body. I'd never seen anyone, let alone my father, look like. . .this. It freaked me out.

The doctor entered and stood still, seeing our shocked expressions.

"You all have to leave. Your father needs his rest." *Rest-schmest.* My father needed me, and I wouldn't leave until he woke up.

Mom looked at the doctor with sad, pleading eyes. "Doctor, have there been any changes?"

Aunt Karen hugged me from behind as I held his hand beside Dad's bed.

"There is nothing else we can do for him at this time but wait."

"Isn't there anything we can do to snap him out of this coma?" I begged.

"Studies have shown patients in a coma can still hear or feel. Piqued emotional interest will be denoted on this monitor. It will tell us if he's on the road to recovery." The doctor considered a moment.

My Mom said quietly, "Howard rarely showed any emotion. The only time I saw him express his emotions was when Max was born. When he took his first breath, I told Howard that we had a healthy baby boy. That's the only time I ever saw him cry." She sounded defeated, but I wouldn't give up. *There had to be a way.*

The doctor escorted us out of the room before turning to Mom. "Your son is too young to be in the room. He'll need to wait in the family lounge."

Damn it! I wasn't too young. I was thirteen fricken years old. I wanted to be there for him like he was there for me. I needed to be there. I was his boychic, and I'd find a way.

"Wait! I want to talk to Dad." I gave his taped and tubed hand a gentle squeeze. In the quietest voice I had ever used, I whispered into his ear, "I love you, Dad. I'll find a way to bring you home. I promise."

I remembered something as we walked back through the halls towards the lounge. It might be nothing, but every idea was a good one at this point. I looked over at Mom. She might remember the same thing.

"Mom. Do you remember the day I came home from baseball practice early?"

"Sure, honey. Your tummy bothered you, but you had to check on Dad first."

"Thank God. You remember it, too." I crossed over to hug her. *Mom had great hugs, too.*

"When I did, I didn't knock on the door like I usually do but went right in. I found Dad sobbing uncontrollably. He motioned me to come in when he saw me, and I stood by his chair. He wiped his face and explained why he was feeling so emotional. It took several minutes for him to calm down.

He pointed to the cassette player on the table and sniffled into a tissue. 'The song you heard was the song

I played for my dad during his last days in hospice. Every time I listen to it, I become an emotional wreck.'"

I sniffled a few times, and his emotions got to me, too.

"Dad explained to me that a good cry can be very healthy and not to be ashamed. I even remember the name of the song that he was listening to. It's called "Monsters," sung by James Blunt. At first, I was upset seeing him crying, but after his explanation, I was moved. We need to go home and listen to that tape. We could bring it over and let him hear it tomorrow." I had a good plan and thank goodness everyone agreed.

The silence on the car ride home was deafening. I didn't care, though. My focus was on two things: finding that tape and listening to it.

29

CHASE AWAY THE MONSTERS

MAX

My family was like a pack of walking zombies as we entered our house. Mom kissed me on my forehead, then crawled up the stairs, and the rest dropped into any available chair or couch to close their eyes. But not me; I was on a mission and knew where to start. I skidded into the den and grabbed the cassette player off the side table. After my tantrum early this morning, Uncle Dale ensured everything was returned to its rightful place. The cassette door was already open, though no tape was inside. Where could it be?

I hurriedly looked all around. I combed through the bookcase, tore through Dad's desk, and even laid on my belly to look under all the furniture. Nothing.

I sat at Dad's desk and leaned way back, my eyes feeling heavy and closing. This morning was like a rollercoaster of ups and downs; if I slept a little, maybe I'd figure out where that tape was.

I was jerked awake by a weird sensation in my chest, and I noticed the sunlight reflecting off something on top of the bookshelf.

I called out to Uncle Dale, who came running. "Max! Are you alright?" He bent over, catching his breath.

"Sorry, Uncle Dale. I didn't mean to scare you. I'm okay. It's just, can you help me grab something up high?"

"Sure, bud, what do you need?"

I pointed at the top of the bookshelf, and he looked at me funny. He left the room and returned with a step stool, trying to reach the object.

"Give me a minute." He took the stool and returned with a ladder. "Why would he place something so high when he knows he can't reach it?" His annoyance at his big brother was obvious. With a final stretch, he palmed the object and handed it down to me. "Here you go."

It was a framed picture of Dad with his dad on a fishing trip. I studied everything in the photo, but when I went to put it down, it rattled. I flipped over the frame and didn't see anything, so I shook it again. *Ah! Inside.* I placed the frame on a flat surface and pried back the fasteners to reveal a cassette tape lodged behind the photo. *Excellent hiding spot, Dad!*

"I found it!"

Uncle Dale stood behind me as I stared at the key to my dad's mystery. I'd found the golden ticket like *Charlie and the Chocolate Factory*. I turned around and hugged my uncle. "I found it," I repeated, and my legs gave out. Uncle Dale dragged me to the oversized, comfy chair and laid a blanket over me.

"Rest up, buddy. You did well today. I'll see you in time for dinner."

"In the morning, we wake up Dad," I said, looking at Uncle Dale.

"We'll see." He kissed my head and left the den, closing the door behind him.

After the Chinese carryout, Mom returned to the hospital for a few hours, and I played a board game with my family. There wasn't anything to do but wait, and we all cashed in early for the night. The cassette tape called me like a siren, but I wanted to listen to it for the first time with my dad, so I forced myself to wait.

Morning couldn't come soon enough. I didn't sleep well, anticipating seeing Dad, yet I stayed in bed until a reasonable hour. Promptly, I went to the kitchen at seven-thirty, grabbed a pot lid and a large spoon, and banged out a loud beat.

"Good morning, Family!" I yelled, dragging out each word.

"What the hell, Max!" Uncle Al left the spare room in the worst boxer shorts ever invented. The rest of them reluctantly came out of their rooms, probably expecting the worst, and that's when I realized I had gone a little overboard with my enthusiasm to start the day.

"Time to go to the hospital! Get it together. We leave in an hour. No ifs, ands, or buts." I commanded, marching back down the stairs. There were moans and groans, but they enabled me, and I appreciated them. I knew they wanted to resolve the big Larry-Howard thing and have my dad wake up from his coma. However, I think they wanted me not to lose my mind waiting for these things to happen. I couldn't agree more.

"Why are we going so early?" Aunt Karen whined.

"Because I found the tape with the song Dad listened to with Grandpa during his last days. This could be the key to waking Dad up. I have to try as soon as possible."

I rushed to grab the cassette player and stuffed the tape inside, fiddling with the buttons. I was a nervous wreck, and I felt all jittery.

"What song was that?" Aunt Karen scoffed. "He never played any music for me. I thought he hated music."

Mom turned to me, "Honey, there's no guarantee that this tape you have such high hopes for will bring your dad back to us."

"The doctor said something could create an emotion that might trigger him to wake up, right? My memory of Dad playing the tape and crying like a baby is the only thing I can think of that could make it happen. Dad asked for a miracle; well, so can I!" I crossed my arms with staunch conviction and determination.

We reached the hospital, checked in at the nursing station, and walked down the long hallway to Dad's room. The staff ignored my age since I was with my family, and we all gathered around his bed as if we were saying a prayer.

The beeps and pings were a steady hum in the background, and outside, there was a constant movement from the doctors and nurses as they went about their business. Dad's chest rose and fell as the machines pushed air into him. I hoped the doctors' plans were working and that my dad's brain would heal. It was time for my miracle to happen, and I motioned for Uncle Dale to shut the door and dim the lights. Carefully, I placed the recorder on the end of Dad's bed and looked at his face. I needed to believe this song would change everything for all of us. We, I, needed my dad back—now.

The crackle and hiss of the ancient recording began, and we lowered our heads, absorbing the frequencies each note delivered. From the very first tone of the song, you can feel the pain and feelings my dad and his father absorbed all those years ago. The lyrics were heartbreaking but soothing at the same time. It became clearer why Dad and his father shared such a special moment. It didn't take long for all of us to start crying. You'd have to be dead inside not to feel the impact of this song—only the one person who needed to feel it didn't move.

The door swung open, and the team of doctors stopped short. You could tell he was assessing everything from the machines to my dad and our faces. Robotically he barked, "We can't have this. Please escort the minor to the lounge and wait. Regardless of the circumstance, only one person may be in the room at a time. My staff will let you know if anything changes."

Wow. What an ass. My Mom was the first to reply. "Have there been any noticeable changes overnight?" Her eyes welled up, waiting for any scrap of good news.

"My team needs to assess your husband's situation, and we can't do that with all these distractions in the room."

"Distractions?!" I yelled directly at this yahoo. "I am trying to save my best friend!" I burst into tears, and my family pushed past these supposed medical geniuses, shuffling me down the hallway and falling defeated into the pleather waiting room seats. That's when the waiting tore into my mind and heart. *Why are they stopping me from being there for him? I knew we made a difference. I was positive!*

Mom placed her hand on top of mine, making circles on my skin to try and soothe me, but I couldn't sit still.

"Mom. I feel him. I sense him. Please, let me go to him after the doctors leave. I'll be quiet as a mouse. No one needs to know I'm in there. Please, Mom." My pleas were pathetic, but I didn't know what else to do.

Mom seemed to understand as she pulled me into a hug. I sat there momentarily, letting her warmth seep into my body. I needed all the love I could get. You don't realize how much of it you want to give to someone until it's moments like these when you fear it might be too late.

I pulled away from the hug, and she knowingly let me go. My head swiveled side-to-side, looking for anyone who might give me resistance, and then we all ran down the hall, dodging the people until I reached Dad's room. I looked behind me before I entered his room and saw my crazy, wonderful family distracting any medical staff, allowing me to slip in unnoticed. Now, *that's what a distraction looks like.* I had my team, and we would make a miracle happen.

I removed the player from my backpack and replayed the tape, cranking the volume louder. I forgot to shut the door when I rushed in, and the music blared down the hall for everyone to hear. The doctor returned to the room, astonished at our disregard for his authority. However, he must have noticed our emotional state and determination and sighed. He turned and walked out of the room without saying a word, closing the door behind him.

"I'm proud of you, boychic," my Uncle Dale announced, patting my shoulder.

"I'll play it as often as it takes to get him to wake up." The emotions in the room felt heavy, even scary. This had to work. *I pressed rewind.* Listen to the song, Dad. *Rewind.* Please think of us, of me! *Rewind.* Damn it, Dad. Wake up! *Rewind.*

Mom saw something move on his face as the song was about to end for the fifth time. The machines started beeping faster, and doctors and nurses rushed into the room.

"Oh, my god..." Mom gasped. I looked from face to face in the room as anguish turned to hope. I faced my father, and our miracle began. A teardrop trickled down his cheek, and I threw myself onto his chest.

"I knew it! I knew it!" I screamed out. "You felt that, didn't you, Dad? That's what you needed. Come on, Dad. We need you to wake up. We need you to live." Each of us let out a sigh of relief followed by hopeful tears.

Both doctors and nurses checked the machines, took his pulse, and tested his reflexes when, finally, the head doctor spoke. "Sounds like he heard you. While I can't give you a definitive answer about when he'll come out of his coma, I can tell you that if his breathing remains constant for the next several hours, we will consider removing his breathing tube." The doctor listened to Dad's chest and took his pulse with his hand instead of the machine's reading. He pressed his lips together and nodded his head confidently. "That's a truly remarkable song. I'll have to remember that one." He patted my shoulder and went back to speaking with the nurse. I was beginning to feel like a dog the way everyone patted me, but I appreciated their compassion.

Something dawned on me. The tape we were listening to had us so immersed in what Dad did for his *dying* father, that we forgot he was still alive! My dad wasn't going to die. I only wanted to shock his system to get an emotional charge, not to make a self-fulfilling prophecy for him.

"Stop playing that song! That's for the dying. And my dad is *not* dying today."

I stormed over and turned off the cassette player.

"I am your Boychic." *No response.*

"I am your Boychic," I repeated louder. Several minutes went by with no response. The other doctors complained we were too loud, and I knew they were going to boot us out of his room again any minute.

"I think it's time for everyone to return to the waiting room. While you've made some progress today, the music is disrupting other patients," he said, resigned.

We were escorted back to the lounge this time, presumably to make sure we made it back there. We waited several more hours waiting to hear if Dad's breathing remained steady. We were emotionally raw yet relieved that we affected him so deeply. I'm sure my Rabbi would be proud of how I prayed. He always told us that the power of prayer, especially as a community, could change the world. I didn't know about the world, but I did know that my prayers would change my dad's life. I was sure of it.

My Mom slung her arm over my shoulders and held me close while Uncle Dale paced. Aunt Karen filed her nails to pass the time, and Uncle Al twiddled his thumbs. I suppose it's times like these that our families' annoyances become iconic traits we'll never forget when they are gone. What silly traits would I remember about my dad? *Nope! Not going there.*

"Mom, please. I want my dad back! Can I go back now? It's been over five hours." My whining had become desperate, but I didn't care. I need to see him *now.*

I didn't wait for her answer and stood up. "Max, sweetheart. The doctors are doing their best, and look, you made a miracle happen in there. Isn't that enough for now?" Her eyes teared up again. I think she feared for my sanity and wouldn't be wrong.

"I have to go back, Mom," I said through teary eyes. She stood again and hugged me, but I didn't need a hug. I needed my dad. I broke Mom's hold and ran back into Dad's room, Mom trailing after me.

"Wait, Max!" She called out.

Dad's siblings' eyes widened as I returned to Dad's room. They knew I'd lost it, but they followed me anyway. Mom slammed into me when I stopped at his room. The tube wasn't attached to his face anymore, and the doctor smiled at the nurse.

"It seems Howard has more living to do, nurse," and looked at us gawking at him. "He's still in a coma but breathing on his own. Hopefully, he will wake up soon." He walked past us, and I didn't wait a minute before throwing myself on his legs.

"Dad! I AM YOUR BOYCHIC! I AM YOUR BOYCHIC!" The past twenty-four hours had been overwhelming. Every nerve in my body was either shocked or sizzling with rage at what happened. I didn't know what else to do.

Mom rubbed my back, "Keep doing what you're doing! Tell that sleepyhead it's time to get up."

I repeated my mantra like I had been *devanning* at Temple. My voice was strained, and I could barely make a sound. Tears streamed down my face, desperation fully taking hold as I slumped again onto the bed. I felt a surge of energy, giving my voice one last prayer, "I can't lose my dad and my best friend at the same time!"

I clawed myself over to the head of the bed, pulling myself close to Dad's side, and held his hand close to my face. I sputtered out one more time, "I am your Boychic." Mom's face looked as bad as mine felt.

My whole family looked like emotional wrecks. When would he listen and wake up?

"It's time for you to rest, sweetheart." She quietly begged me to stop. I turned to Dad one last time before they dragged me away again. Our family barricade was broken, and the doctors and nurses busted through. I couldn't fight them anymore. I did what I could and would have to come to terms with whatever the outcome.

I slowly let them walk me out of the room when I saw a familiar ghostly figure in the corner. It was the same man I saw at my dad's birthday party. Could this be my miracle wish, too? I pleaded to the heavens. This was my last-ditch effort to make my miracle happen, and I opened my mouth to say, "I—I am your-"

"Boychic." Dad finished the sentence. His voice was clear as day. Ten people did an about-face in unison as my dad opened his eyes slowly. I rushed forward to take his hand as he lifted his to my head. "You are my BOYCHIC."

The doctor and nurses couldn't believe what they had just witnessed—a genuine miracle. "I gave one back to you for all the miracles you've done for me." Everyone was filled with joy, and tears ran down their faces. Mom rushed over to give Dad a big hug and a smile.

"I'm so glad you're awake." Tears welled once more, and she hugged Aunt Karen. The other siblings crowded around, scolding my dad for creating the accident in the first place, but overall, it's a nice thing to see. Dad smiled at me from the bed and nodded. I may never know Dad completely, but I would always know I loved him. He beckoned me over and I gave him a big bear hug.

"I'm glad you're awake, Dad," I said softly, my voice still ripped to horrific shreds.

"I'm glad I'm here for you, too, boychic." He smiled. Everyone was exhausted. The family, the nurse staff, the doctor, everyone.

The doctor sighed, "We will need to keep him for several days and watch his progress, but all signs point to a full recovery. In the meantime, if everyone can go home and get some rest. We'll call if anything changes. He needs rest—lots of rest."

Everyone hugged the doctor, leaving him looking flustered. I hugged my dad tightly, promising to be back soon. His pained grimace was a reminder that he had also broken his arm and not to squeeze him so tight next time.

Uncle Al didn't miss a beat, "Does anyone have a marker so I can sign this clown's cast? 'To Howard or Larry, who the hell knows...'"

"Now that your dad looks like he will be on the mend, what are your plans for the next few weeks?" Uncle Dale remarked.

I pondered the question, looked at Uncle Dale, Aunt Karen, Uncle Al, and Mom, and smiled. "I think I will teach myself how to ride a bike."

* *devanning – deep prayer*

30

HOLD ON TIGHT

HOWARD

Ten days after I woke up, I was finally released from the hospital. Those doctors put me through the wringer, and they wouldn't stop anytime soon. Physical therapy, occupational therapy, and regular checkups kept me busy for months. Me and my rideshare driver became good friends since I couldn't drive on my own for the next month.

I was messed up pretty badly, and that came with a good talking to myself about my obsessive nature. My desire to be Max's best friend almost got me killed. It was enough to be his father—and maybe a bit more. My plans to improve my perfect putter stroke went out the window, as did expanding my business to the East Coast. All my immediate plans began and ended in my backyard.

Beyond my physical ailments, things slowly began to return to normal. Max became a helpful, appreciative, and cheery son. That alone made for a more pleasant existence. Dale must have given everyone a rundown of what transpired before, during, and after I got home from camp. For Max, though, he must have discussed how desperate I was to fix our relationship and to what lengths I'd go to be his friend. Max treated me better and even went out of his way, offering to spend time with me. *I'd have to send Dale a note and a gift card to his favorite place.*

Ilene was back at work, though the smile on her face every morning was bigger and brighter than I'd ever seen before. She told me I was in trouble for putting her through that ordeal and was banned from rollerblades forever. I knew she was scared, and I did everything I could to ease her suffering by being compliant through my therapies. By the end of September, I would have the keys back to my car, and I could resume taking Max out for ice cream or going out for a walk unchaperoned. The realization that time stopped for no one led me to appreciate every moment of my life and how I chose to spend it. Max was growing up, and I'd do better to allow him to take the wheel of his life than drive it for him.

I approached Max, who was dribbling a soccer ball for his school's team tryouts. "I still have my rollerblades in the garage and would love to go blading with you." I leaned against the backyard door wall, *kvelling* over his laughter and incredulous face.

"The only way you get to go blading with me is if I can double-wrap you in bubble wrap." We both burst out laughing at that image.

"Fine. What are your terms, Cap'n?" I said, saluting him seriously.

Max rolled his eyes back. "I will tie a rope onto the back of my bike and get you up to speed that you can enjoy the experience fully."

"You know how to ride a bike?" I asked, bewildered.

"Sure do." He said without looking at the ball, bouncing off his knees. "I taught myself while you were recovering from your accident."

"You did? That's amazing, Max. I'm so proud of you. I walked over and hugged him. "I'm going to take you up on that as soon as the doctor releases me for full activity." I hugged him again and ran into the house to call my doctor.

Two weeks later, Max was rigging his bike to haul my ass down the street. I looked like the Michelin Man the way he wrapped me in pads and donned a new customized helmet named "Larry" in block letters on one side and "Pitbull" on the other. It was the best gift ever! He ensured that my rollerblades were snapped down properly and insisted we first practice stopping safely. *Now, why didn't I think of that?*

"Safety first, Larry." He smacked his thigh and bent over backward, cracking himself up. It was funny. Thank goodness we're past all that trauma.

"One last thing before we start," Max said, running inside the garage and pulling out two pool noodles and some duct tape.

"Are we going rollerblading, or are you having a German Shepherd attack dog have his way with me?"

Max clapped. "You're still recovering, and I'd be liable if you got hurt on my watch. Remember, we can't tell Mom what we're doing." He stepped back hysterically, seeing his work. He had me covered from head to toe. Max tied a rope to the back of his bike and handed me the end of it.

"It's time to fly." He jumped on his bike, stood on the pedals to get us going, and headed down the driveway onto the street. This is what I'd been praying for—another adventure and making memories with my son.

"That's a great-looking bike."

"It was the most expensive one they had in the store. It's gotta be good!"

We checked frequently for traffic as we glided past our friends' homes. The freedom I felt as the air blew into my face was exhilarating.

"Can't you pedal any faster? I feel you're taking me for a drag rather than flying." Suffice it to say my sarcasm didn't suffer from my injury.

"Hold on, old man. You want fast? Buckle up because here you go!" Max stood on his pedals again, pumping as hard as he could, making his bike lean left and right with his exertion.

As we approached a major intersection, fun shifted to fear. Feelings of deja vu flooded my body as I calculated the velocity of how I would swing out as we turned. *Breathe, Howard.*

"Hey, Max," I called out. You might want to slow down a little! We are coming up to a wide curve." Max ignored my warning and pressed harder on his pedals, making us go faster and faster. I held on as tightly as I could, managing to hold on. That was until Max lost his focus. I followed his gaze and saw the group of ladies jogging by.

Max laughed about what I didn't know.

"Hey, Dad. Check out those women jogging over there. Quality FTBs."

In his moment of teen weakness, he lost control and swung me out too far. I flew into the air and hit the ground, rolling into a hedge of bushes. Max stopped and jumped off his bike, screaming my name as he ran toward me.

"Dad! Dad! Are you okay?" The worry on his face was priceless. I was lying on my belly in the middle of a bunch of bushes, and I struggled to lift my head. I groaned, spitting leaves from my mouth. I raised my hand with a thumbs-up and dropped my head to the side. Full of adrenaline and joy that I was still alive, I triumphantly lifted my head and yelled, "Max! YOU SON OF A BOYCHIC!"

THE END

A WORD ABOUT RELATIONSHIPS

Our relationships are everything and in so many ways, they define the very core of our humanity. In Jewish tradition, it is paramount to God that individuals and families figure out how to get it right with one another. This includes doing whatever is in our power to reconcile strained and broken relationships. And we can engage in this process of repair as long as there is breath left in our bodies. As a hospice rabbi, one of my greatest challenges is assisting people in finding a pathway toward reconnecting with their loved ones at end of life. But thankfully, we don't have to wait that long to seek forgiveness and understanding!

In 'A Father's Wish, ' Howard Emmer brilliantly weaves a most beautiful, thoughtful, and inspiring story of a father and son who have grown apart- as many parents and children do- both in their younger years and in their older ones. Howard's profound wish to reconnect with Max is unyielding. He goes to great lengths and takes the extreme steps that he deems essential, leading to a heart-warming journey of understanding, compassion, and empathy forged between father and son. This is a story that transcends the generations and shows how much and how deeply we really, truly need each other.

Rabbi Joseph H. Krakoff

CEO, Jewish Hospice and Chaplaincy Network (JHCN)

ABOUT HOWARD

Rooted in family and spirituality, Howard L. Emmer released his creative side in his first book, A Father's Wish. Born in California, he learned to hustle and became a self-made man. After meeting Ilene on a blind date in California, they decided to get married and move back to Michigan, where Ilene was originally from. Love and laughter have always been at the forefront of his life, as well as the desire to see the world. Meeting new people and discovering their cultures has created many paths to personal growth and a strong moral code. You can find Howard's book on Amazon in a variety of formats.

Howard's Inspiration

I was the father of a teenage son who couldn't fathom why we drifted apart. We did everything together—until he became a teenager—and that was when this book was born.

Later in life, my son, Max, married and had his own son, Rocky. Max opened up to me when his own son was only two years old. He questioned himself, wondering if he could ever be as good a father as I was to him. I was astounded by his lack of confidence, knowing that both his family and friends saw in action what a great dad he was. I always felt proud of my son and thanked my spirits above that he had grown up to be a great man, husband, and father.

I was positive my father's way was the best way and pressed upon my son the decades-old lessons my father taught me, eventually realizing they weren't best for him or for myself. My exploration didn't stop there. Like a newborn opening its eyes for the first time, I saw how controlling and stubborn I had become throughout the years, like my dad, and I made the decision to cleanse myself of this way of thinking for good.

Whether it's a father's or mother's wish, I believe every parent and child can seek their own insights on improving, enjoying, and growing healthy relationships with their children without bringing bad baggage along the journey.

Max is now thirty-five years old, and I couldn't be prouder of this amazing man. Fly, Max, and let this stubborn dad follow along for the ride.

BONUS LINKS

Do you want to hear the music Max played for his dad?
And what Howard and his father listened in his final hours?
Click on the below link or visit YouTube and type in
Monsters by James Blunt
https://www.youtube.com/watch?v=DTFbGcnl0po

As a special thank you, to you, my readers, I will make a donation for each book purchased towards the MAKE-A-WISH Foundation at Wish.org

or for eBook Readers, click on the below link:
Make-A-Wish Foundation Direct Donation Link

ACKNOWLEDGEMENTS

To my wife Ilene ~ who, after 40+ years of marriage, still lifts my spirits, inspires my creativity, and enriches my life. Thank you for putting up with all my luggage. You truly are the one who has done the heavy lifting, and I will always love you for that.

To my son Max ~ your accomplishments speak for themselves, but seeing how you respect and help others and open your heart to them makes me so proud to be your father.

To Caryn ~ Thank you for being the daughter I never had, a loving wife to Max, and a caring and adoring mother to Rocky. You are the perfect addition to our family, and I will be forever grateful for that.

To my grandson Rocky ~ I already see at your very young age, the gleam in those gorgeous baby blue eyes and your contagious laughter, that you are and will be another son of a Boychic. I hope I am here long enough to see your growth, become a young man, and spoil you as much as possible.

To my dad ~ who passed way too early at the age of 57. I miss you every day, and how I wish you could have played with your grandson Max. He has grown into such an excellent man, husband, and father.

To my mother ~ whose sense of humor wasn't always understood by many, but I got it, and I love you for it.

To my siblings ~ I always found jobs for you wherever I worked, and you promptly got us all fired. Our memories together growing up will always be times that I'll cherish. I'm looking forward to many more years of friendship.

To Samantha and Cindy ~ I wrote my first book about special father and son relationships. It became very clear after meeting both of you that your daughter-mother team shared a similar bond as I did with my son. Though I wasn't blessed with a daughter, it warmed my heart to see how you both worked together to help and guide me through this writing journey. Our journey together became like that of a close-knit family of friends I could enjoy for years. We enjoyed crafting a meaningful story while laughing and crying together as we breathed life into these pages. Thank you for making my dream come true.